A SIERRA THE SEARCH DOG NOVEL

PAYOUT

THE SCENT OF MONEY

Sarah —
Stay Found!
[signature]

ROBERT D. CALKINS

Payout -- *The Scent of Money*

A Sierra the Search Dog Novel

By Robert D. Calkins

Callout Press

Published by Callout Press, Olalla, Washington, U.S.A.

Copyeditor: Lisa Canfield

Proofreader: Lisa Canfield

Cover: AJ Canfield

Interior Design: Callout Press

ISBN: 978-0-9971911-5-8

Library of Congress Control Number: 2018906125

Dedicated to Amber Ale, Sierra's mother and the beautiful Golden Retriever who started it all.

Acknowledgements

There is one group that is too-often forgotten when authors of true crime or procedural fiction present acknowledgements: the victims and their families.

For a search and rescue team to have a professionally rewarding experience, some other individual must be having a very bad day. By extension, that missing subject's family, loved ones and friends are also having very bad days.

This book, with some creative license, is the product of many searches for many missing subjects on behalf of many worried families. It is not the author's intent to profit from their pain. It is the author's intent that this work of fiction honor those who search in the spirit of the search and rescue motto:

THAT OTHERS MIGHT LIVE.

Chapter One

Trust your dog

There dogs that search, and then there are search dogs.

Dogs that search are told when it's time to work. The handler puts a harness or vest on the dog, gives a voice command or perhaps a hand signal and the dog begins searching. Dogs that search do fine work and produce excellent results—when they're searching.

Search dogs, on the other hand, are like that irritating friend who's always "on." They're searching the driveway on the way to the car. They're searching the car on the way to the vet. They're searching the vet's waiting room. If there's a dead body in the lobby, a search dog will find it. No cueing is needed. No vest, nor voice command. Search dogs search, all the time.

Sierra was a search dog.

On this day, however, Sierra was a search dog who needed to potty…and wouldn't.

"C'mon, Sierra. Will ya just go? I know you hate going on-leash, but there's just too much traffic to let you run loose."

he leash came from Sierra's human,
:am. Bryce Finn had only recently
a fixture in the search and rescue
iough, the two weren't supposed to
l the rest of the Finn family for what
quiet dinner at the home of Bryce's

repeatedly with her nose almost touching the grass. Suddenly she shot forward toward a white SUV parked crookedly at the curb. Bryce's shoulder nearly left its socket.

"Whoa, girl! Whatcha got?" Sierra answered by pulling even harder. Her breathing got louder and more rhythmic. Her tail stood straight up and stiff, swinging like a metronome as she dragged Bryce toward the parked vehicle.

She sniffed the passenger door first, paying special attention to the handle that someone likely had touched. She snorted to clear her nasal passages, and then drew in a big breath of air. She lowered her nose, and moved forward from the door—still sniffing—almost to the bumper. Finally, she slowed her pace then sat, quietly, staring intently at right front fender.

The official name for what Sierra had done was a "trained final response." It was her dead-bang-rock-solid-no-doubt-whatsoever message that she'd found decaying human tissue. But if Sierra was intent, Bryce was confused. Why would his very reliable search dog alert on a random car fender? Sure, the car could have run over an animal, but Bryce had spent many hours training Sierra NOT to alert on dead mice, dead rabbits, dead cats…or anything at all except dead humans. So why the fender of this car, on this street, on this day?

A screen door slammed.

"Honey, are you about done?" his mother called. "We're ready for dessert. Hasn't Sierra 'done her business' yet?"

"She's on to something here," Bryce replied. "I have no idea why, but I can't pull her off this car fender. You all go ahead. I want to let her figure this out."

Bryce's mom rolled her eyes, but didn't argue. History had proved that neither her son nor his dog would relax until there was an explanation for Sierra's alert. Her son would just have to get his dessert whenever he got around to it.

"Whatcha got, girl?" Bryce asked again. He didn't want to correct her, in case there really was something human on the fender. He couldn't imagine what it might be, but he'd learned long ago that Sierra was a dog he could trust. Some dogs will give false alerts hoping to get their reward toy. But while Sierra was psychotic for her tennis ball, she had never once tried to cheat.

Sierra continued to stare, and Bryce's eyes followed hers. Looking more closely at the car, he realized something was amiss. The fender was off, skewed slightly. The gap between the fender and the hood wasn't uniform, and the top of the bumper and the fender didn't meet correctly. Upon further inspection Bryce saw that the fancy headlight lens, with all its shiny LED bulbs, had a very small crack in it.

"This car's hit something...or someone," he thought. Then it clicked. Two nights before he'd walked into the family living room, and caught just a snippet of a TV news story. All he could remember was "hit and run," and "white SUV."

"Good girl," he said to Sierra, very gently. Because he wasn't sure if the dog was correct yet, he kept the praise to a minimum and walked her away from the car. His call to 9-1-1 was answered on the first ring.

"9-1-1, what are you reporting?" asked the operator, in a very stern voice.

"Hi, it's Bryce Finn from Search and Rescue. I'm calling about a suspicious car."

The dispatcher's tone changed immediately. "Bryce! It's Marilyn. How's our county's youngest search dog handler? More importantly, how is that sweet puppy of yours?"

"Sierra's fine, ma'am. But we're both a little confused. She's given me a solid cadaver alert on a car fender that has some damage. I remember something about a hit-and-run a couple nights ago. The suspect vehicle is a white SUV."

"Oh God, I took the call from that man's wife," Marilyn replied. "I had nightmares from her screams. If you've found the car I'm going to kiss both you AND that dog! You said a white SUV, right?"

"Yes. I can give you a plate."

"Go ahead."

Bryce read her the license plate number and gave a full description of both the vehicle and the damage.

"The wife never got the plate, but everything else matches," Marilyn said. "They were walking along the road, so it was the right front fender that clipped him."

Bryce knew they were onto something. "That's where Sierra alerted. Are you going to have a deputy come out?"

"Nope," the dispatcher said. "I'm going straight to the detective on the case. It's Lenora Hogan—this is a pretty solid lead and I think she'll want to handle this herself. Can I have her call you?"

"Of course," Bryce replied.

"In the meantime you be careful. If the owner's around he might freak at all the attention. Is there someplace safe where you can keep an eye on the vehicle?"

"No problem. We're visiting family over here. I'm due for dessert, so I can watch from the kitchen window. I'll call back if anybody starts to get in."

* * *

Bryce was inside, and about halfway through a piece of chocolate cheesecake when his phone rang. The caller didn't bother to identify herself.

"If you've found the car I'm going to kiss both you and that dog."

Detective Hogan had led a couple of searches that Bryce had been on. She'd always treated him and the other SAR volunteers with great respect. To his knowledge, she'd never offered to kiss any of them.

Bryce laughed. "That's what Marilyn said—between the two of you I'll end up in trouble with Katie. You want to come look at the car?"

"Already on the way."

"Is it registered nearby?" Bryce asked. "Marilyn was worried the suspect might notice all the fussing around."

"Not even close," the detective replied. "Marilyn did a really nice workup on the plate. It's registered over on Lakeview Avenue, but the house number puts it in the middle of Wildcat Lake. The listed owner doesn't have a phone, driver's license, criminal history, pay taxes or own property in Kitsap County."

"You mean it's a cold car?" Bryce was incredulous.

"Ice cold. Even if it's not our hit and run suspect, it's still an interesting car. We'll solve a crime today, whether it's my case or somebody else's."

"I'll be here," Bryce answered. He tried to force down the last few bites of cheesecake, but his mind was racing. What were the chances that somebody went to all the trouble to completely hide ownership of a car, for some totally unrelated reason, only to *accidentally* run over a pedestrian?

The answer was obvious.

Sierra hadn't found the suspect vehicle in some random hit and run. She'd found a murder weapon.

Chapter Two
Cha-Ching!

This cash register didn't make the usual noise.

That's because the sound of a body bouncing off rocks while en-route to the bottom of a cliff doesn't jingle or jangle. It makes a series of dull plopping sounds…at least once the screams stop.

The conversation had begun innocently enough. "Thanks for inviting me up here," the man said. "I've never spent much time in the woods and this view is awesome."

"Don't get to close to the edge," the other man replied, his voice oozing concern. He'd gotten to know his victim just well enough to predict what would happen next.

"I'm not afraid of heights. I even clean my own…"

And those were the last words Jason Manley ever spoke. Well, besides the screams. A gentle nudge was all it took, and gravity finished the job.

As Manley went over, his pack briefly scuffed the dirt at the edge of the cliff. "Perfect," his killer thought. A clue for the police. For the plan to work, someone had to eventually find the body.

The trip back to the trailhead took about 40 minutes. That gave him time to calm down, restore his breathing and get his story straight. Even for someone who'd killed many times, the actual act always triggered a rush of adrenalin. Experience told him to be appropriately calm, no, *concerned*, before he called police.

After more thought, he decided to wait before calling 9-1-1. Instead, he spent some time at the trailhead building a background story. "Have you seen my friend?" he asked several people coming off the trail. "We got separated and he hasn't shown back up."

No one had seen anything, but that didn't matter. The point was to contact enough people to have witnesses to his *concern*. Once he did, it was time to make the call.

"9-1-1, what are you reporting?"

"I'm over on Green Mountain, and my friend is missing off the Tin Mine Trail," he responded. "We were hiking and got separated, and he hasn't come back."

First he'd wait for the police. Then, he'd wait for his payout.

Chapter Three

On the Breeze

"What's the problem here?" Bryce asked.

Katie didn't know. Her dog Magnum was going nuts in a patch of hip-deep western Washington underbrush. He was running back and forth, and had shifted from snorting to whining—a sign that he was frustrated at not having found their hidden subject.

Bryce had always been grateful to Sierra for bringing him together with Katie. Now, Sierra's little brother was putting a strain on that relationship.

"What's Magnum doing?" Bryce pressed. He knew exactly what baby brother was doing, because he'd set up the training. That training included peppering Katie with questions to mimic the stress of a real search.

"He's frustrated!" Katie replied. "I am too. Alissa's gotta be right here, but we're not finding her." Like many new dog handlers, Katie's desire to succeed left her open to emotion, which has no place in search and rescue. Human emotions flow right down the leash, and can affect the dog's performance.

"Run 'im up toward the ridgeline there," Bryce gently suggested.

"I've done that!" Katie snapped. "Every time we go that way, he loses scent. She's gotta be right here!"

"Run him up to the TOP of that ridgeline," Bryce suggested, a bit less gently. They were on the southern slope of Green Mountain, and there was always a ridgeline someplace.

"OK...if you say so..."

Katie started up the hill, and Magnum reluctantly followed. Twice he returned to the patch of brush at the bottom and made circles. Twice Katie called Magnum back, and directed him up the slope ahead of her. So she was pretty surprised that when Magnum finally reached the top, his nose went up and he quickly disappeared from view.

"Aw jeez..." was all Katie had time to mumble.

In short order Magnum came flying straight down the hill to Katie. He tried to sit, but the combination of the steep slope and his own momentum transformed Magnum's trained response into a klutzy somersault. But Katie recognized the effort, and gave the appropriate command.

"Show me!"

Magnum righted himself and was gone in a flash. In a few seconds his incessant barking could be heard from just over the ridgeline. It didn't take much to figure out how to speak dog. "Found 'em! Time for my paycheck! Where's my ball, you slowpoke human? Bark bark bark!"

Katie caught up, and saw that their subject was hidden in some brush about 50 feet back from the lip of the ravine. She tossed

Magnum that paycheck—an orange rubber ball with a squeaker inside.

"Yayyy Magnum! Whatagooddogyoufoundemyoufoundem!" she cried. "Alissa, thanks so much for hiding for us. I'm completely confused about how you're up here instead of down there, but I suspect we'll both get a lesson in a moment."

The training problem had indeed been a frustrating one for Katie. What had just happened? Had Magnum given a completely false alert at the bottom of the hill? Still, Katie saw to it that her dog got plenty of reward before they stopped to discuss the issue. She tossed his ball, offered him praise and water, scratched his butt and rubbed his belly. She did a good job of making him feel like the best dog in the world.

But underneath it all, Bryce could see that Katie was wrung out.

Bryce offered reassurance. "Your dog wasn't wrong, and wasn't bluffing you," he explained. "Check the wind." Only months older than Katie, he had become her mentor, and she his student...his "Grasshoppah."

Katie brought out a simple nasal spray bottle refilled with plain water. She spritzed it into the air and saw that the wind was blowing directly off the edge of the plateau, toward the ravine where they'd been so confused.

"But why didn't he follow the scent up here?" she asked, continuing to toss Magnum's ball as she spoke. "He turned around every time we started up the hill."

"Human scent is heavier than air, but not by much," Bryce explained. "The wind blew the scent over the edge and into the ravine, but it didn't flow straight downhill like water. The wind carried it out further, and *then* it fell."

"So there's a gap…?" The light was starting to come on.

"We call it a 'skip zone,'" Bryce said. "The scent skips over one area and then lands in another. You wind up with a big ol' pool of scent down at the bottom of the hill, but nothing along the slope itself."

Katie's shoulders slumped and she looked at her feet. Bryce realized he needed to turn a frustrating training evolution into a positive experience for her. The good news was, he didn't need to sugarcoat or lie.

"Something very good happened here. You just can't see it 'cuz you're bummed."

"…And that would be…?" Katie asked, in a tone about halfway between annoyed and skeptical.

"You can tell when your dog is and isn't in scent. Do you know how many handlers have washed out over that? Yes, you needed to learn a lesson about terrain and how scent moves on the wind. Fundamentally, though, you read your dog correctly. You did great."

"But I feel like such an idiot. We were less than a hundred feet from Alissa and had no idea she was here!"

"Trust me, this won't be the last time you feel like an idiot. We all do. I promise, the best way to get through it is by doing what I just said: trust Magnum and trust yourself."

Bryce decided it was time to change the subject.

"Why don't I get Sierra out of the truck and we all hike out the GM4 Road?" Bryce offered. "Alissa, you're welcome to come along if you have time. We can go to Lost Creek or maybe a bit beyond. The dogs can play in the water and we can call it a conditioning hike for us human types.

"That sounds like a good idea," Katie replied. "I've had enough stress for one day."

"I'd love to come along," Alissa chimed in. "This is all so fascinating. I wish I had time to work a dog, but I'll just have to get my fix with puppy kisses."

Alissa had joined SAR as a "support member," meaning she didn't have a dog of her own but would accompany dog teams on searches, helping with navigation, radio communication and other tasks.

It didn't take long to get Sierra and head back out for the 45 minute walk to Lost Creek. As they walked, Bryce and Katie shifted the subject to plans for their regular Saturday night date. That led to discussion of plans for Sunday, and the school week coming up.

"You two sound like an old married couple," Alissa said. "You have this casual comfort between you like you've been together forever. You sound just like my husband and me planning our week, figuring out who's cooking dinner and who's picking up the kids."

Bryce and Katie didn't know what to make of the comment. "Well, at least we don't have any kids to worry about," Katie finally stammered as a response.

"Not yet, anyway," Bryce added.

Katie's face reddened. "Did you really say that? Are you planning that someday, we…?"

It was one of those moments when a girl hopes for a romantic response that will sweep her off her feet. And at that moment, just like in the movies, music began to play.

But this wasn't a romantic tune. And it wasn't the first time this particular tune had interrupted a romantic moment.

"Rescue Me!" cried Aretha Franklin's unmistakable, bluesy voice. It was the ringtone on Bryce's phone, the special one he'd set to play only when the call was for a search. He answered just as the Queen of Soul was imploring someone to take her in their arms.

"This is an alert from Kitsap County Search and Rescue," the recorded voice said. "We have an overdue male hiker on the Tin Mine Trail at Green Mountain. Base will be at the Gold Creek Trailhead. Ground pounders and K9s needed."

"We're on the wrong side of the mountain," Katie realized. "We need to get back to the rigs."

"I've got a better idea," Bryce said. "Let's hike over the top."

"But that'll take forever," Alissa interjected.

"It's called containment. If the subject headed off on the wrong trail, he could be coming our way. About the only place to get lost off the Tin Mine is the road we're already on. He might be headed straight for us."

"Well, I'm up for that," Katie said. "But is Magnum allowed to come on searches?"

"It's not really a K9 assignment," Bryce pointed out. "We'll just walk toward Gold Creek and see if we bump into the guy."

Bryce phoned the SAR unit leader to let him know what they were up to, and the unusual arrangement was quickly approved. The three humans and two canines set off toward Lost Creek, and from there up the mountain to Horse Camp. Bryce figured that if the missing subject had found his way there, the composting toilet and picnic shelter might keep him around waiting for help.

Lost Creek was in its springtime rage, churning with runoff from the winter snowmelt. The dogs didn't mind, though, and all three humans managed to cross without overtopping their boots. Then it was up the hill toward Horse Camp, to find an equestrian group spending the day.

"We've been here since sunup...haven't seen the guy," said the woman cleaning up behind her mare. "If he shows up here who should we call?"

"9-1-1" was Bryce's answer. "Just let them know he's at Horse Camp and we'll send somebody."

From Horse Camp, the terrain dropped down the south side of Green Mountain to where the trail eventually split. A logging road led to Gold Creek Trailhead, while a very rocky trail went back up a small spur to the higher Tin Mine Trail. That's where Bryce and Katie had to go their separate ways.

"Base, Dog 44" was Bryce's call over the radio.

"Dog 44, good to have you in radio range. Any luck on your trip over the top?" came the reply from the command post.

"Negative. Not a thing. The folks at Horse Camp were advised and will keep a lookout for him. We're currently at the split between the GM4 and the Creek Trail. Katie and Magnum are going to walk the road into base. I'm taking Alissa as field support and we're headed 'up the Creek,' so to speak. We'll let you know when we get to the intersection with Tin Mine."

"Sounds like a plan," the base operator replied. *"One of the other handlers has a spare crate for Magnum. We'll send Katie out as support for them."*

"Sounds good. 44 clear," Bryce signed off.

"Base clear," was the response.

During certain times of the year, the Creek Trail really was a creek. This was one of those times. Bryce and Alissa were in six inches of water, walking on slick rocks, hoping not to roll an ankle. Sierra, on the other hand, was in Golden Retriever heaven. She was able to play in the water and do her job at the same time. About half-way to the Tin Mine Trail they got a radio call from Katie.

"44, 66."

Just from her tone Bryce could tell something was wrong. "44, go ahead," he said in a voice he hoped would calm Katie.

"This is 66. Magnum's just jumped in the swamp and is heading your way. He won't come back. Looks like he's trying to hook back up with you and Sierra."

"Well if he's in the swamp he's way ahead of us," Bryce radioed back. "We're not to the Tin Mine yet and the swamp is below that. You sure he's not just playing in the water? If he's trying to get to us, he'll never get up the cliff."

"He's definitely not just playing in the water. He's making a beeline toward the cliff, running where it's shallow, swimming where he has to...wait, he's coming back."

Magnum approached Katie and didn't bother to shake the muddy water off like most dogs. He ran directly up to her and sat.

"C'mon, Magnum, let's go" Katie ordered as she turned to continue walking down the road. "We gotta get to base."

Magnum ran around in front of Katie and sat again, this time looking her right in in the eye. When she tried to go around him a second time, Magnum put both front paws on her thighs and pushed her back. He continued staring directly into her eyes and never even blinked. When Katie got back on the radio, Bryce could hear her frustration.

"44, 66. First he came back and sat in front of me. When I tried to go around him he jumped up and pushed me back."

"He sat..." was Bryce's reply, his voice trailing off. He un-keyed his microphone and thought for a moment. He didn't want to embarrass Katie over the radio, but he had to say it.

"Your dog just came back from the base of a cliff, and sat in front of you. That might be something you'd want to check out. Maybe you could try saying the phrase that pays."

Katie turned to Magnum. "Show me?" she tried, more as a question than a command.

Magnum immediately turned and bolted back into the shallow swamp. He was soon out of sight, and only a short time later was barking the same incessant bark Katie had heard on their training search.

Katie began trying to pick her own way through the swamp. She could step on tufts of grass that would keep most of the water out of her boots. She literally hopped and skipped her way through the watery terrain, homing in on the sound of Magnum's barking.

"He's right at the base of the cliff," Katie radioed to Bryce. *"I'm almost…"* and the transmission cut off.

"66, you still with us?" Bryce called. "66?"

"66, this is Base. Do you read us?"

No response.

"Base, 44. You got anybody else close?" Bryce chimed in. "I don't like that we've lost contact with a lone handler in a swamp."

"Base here…we agree. Can you make your way back down to the road? We've got another team we can divert that way."

Bryce's radio squealed a bit, the way radios do when two stations transmit at once. It meant someone was trying to break into his conversation with Base. Bryce hesitated before speaking again, and his patience was rewarded.

"This is 66, do you copy?" Katie repeated, frustration audible in her voice. *"We've bumped into Nat Sessions' team…and…and we're going to…take a break with them."*

Death code. Katie had just found a body.

Nat Sessions had been a beloved member of SAR, and was long deceased. Searchers used Nat's name to report finding a body, to keep the discovery at least temporarily a secret. They wanted families to hear that most awful of news from a chaplain or sheriff's deputy, not a reporter with a police scanner.

Katie knew she sounded rattled on the radio, and tried to regain her composure.

"So, Magnum was just smelling Nat, that's why he came into the swamp," was her next transmission. *"We're fine."*

"66, Base. Do you have coordinates on where you've...um...bumped into Nat?"

"Sure, give me a sec," came Katie's voice back, very casually. She was sounding more comfortable. She got out her GPS unit, which would translate her location into a series of letters and numbers.

"OK, Base...here you go. Coordinates follow: 10-Tango 0535161. Next line 5266919."

Bryce, Sierra and Alissa were now hurrying back down the Creek Trail, heading for the intersection where they'd split from Katie and Magnum. "This is 44," he said. "I think there's an overgrown road that skirts the base of the cliff. It's barely still there, but if Alissa and I can find it through the brush we can get to you with dry feet.

"This is Base. We've got a couple more teams that'll stage out on that road. We'll wait for the coroner before we take the stretcher in."

Bryce made a mental note to talk to the base radio operator. There was no point in having a death code if the follow-up transmissions made reference to the coroner. But he'd worry about that later. He, Alissa and Sierra had found the abandoned logging road, and were headed toward Katie's location.

* * *

The crumpled body was twisted grotesquely from the fall, the neck obviously broken. "At least he didn't suffer," Bryce thought. Sierra had blown past Katie and Magnum to the body, and returned to give her own alert. Even though the remains had already been officially "found" by Magnum, they were fresh to Sierra and she did her job. Bryce tossed Sierra's ball away from the body, to keep her clear. Although he figured the fall was likely accidental, the area would initially be considered a crime scene.

"Base, 44. We're with 66 waiting for the other teams. From base they need to go on down and catch that overgrown road I mentioned. We tied yellow survey ribbon on a branch so they'll know where to look for it."

"44, Base...roger that. We've got a deputy coming with the team to stand by for the coroner. As soon as he's there you can return to base."

"44 understood," Bryce repeated back. "Once the deputy's here we'll RTB and get this written up. Out."

"Base clear."

"Sooo...Katie, how ya gonna write this up?" Bryce tried to ask in the lightest possible tone. It would be Katie's job to provide a full written report on how Jason Manley's body was located and what she found at the scene.

"I don't know," Katie replied. "We weren't even really searching. Magnum's not certified yet. Am I in trouble?"

"You are most definitely not in trouble," Bruce replied emphatically. "It was all approved in advance. Nobody could have known your path would take you downwind of a dead body. In fact, you're probably going to get some pats on the back. Which takes us back to my question: how are you going to write this up?"

"We were just walking along the road when Magnum jumped in the swamp, came back and sat," Katie offered meekly. "It never occurred to me that he'd located our subject."

"Well, don't put that part in your report," Bryce warned. "Just say you were walking along the road when your dog gave you a 'trained final response' you weren't expecting, and you followed up."

* * *

Katie had seen enough of Bryce's reports to know what to write, but she was still rattled. It was one thing to leave base knowing that you're looking for a body. It's quite another to be surprised by one without any mental prep.

As Katie wrote, she glanced out the window and saw Bryce talking with the deputy and Gary Manning, their SAR team leader. Maybe Bryce thought she wasn't in trouble, but were others unhappy? Was Bryce being questioned for his judgment in walking over the mountain? Was he taking a bullet for her?

She finished the report and handed it to the operations chief. Just as she stepped out of the command van, she saw Manning heading her way.

"This is it," she thought. "This is where I get my rear-end chewed for searching when I wasn't supposed to."

"Hey, Katie," Manning called. "If you're all done with that report, I need to chat with you for a minute."

It all came spilling out.

"I'm so sorry," Katie blurted. "I didn't think we were searching. We were just walking back to base and Magnum took off. I didn't even realize he'd given me an alert at first…"

"Katie…"

"No, please, this is my fault. I should have controlled him better. What if this turns out to be a crime and an uncertified dog was inside the scene? And don't be mad at Bryce. I mean...he did check with you first. He just didn't know..."

"Katie...STOP!" Manning had to raise his voice. "You're not in trouble."

"I'm not?" came the very thin, meek reply.

"It WAS all approved in advance. I'm the one who okayed it, so if anyone has a problem they can come to me," Manning said. "Now, let's get to the real reason I wanted to talk. I have some news for you."

"Okayyy?"

"We all agreed that Magnum did a great job finding the body, and once you got over the initial surprise, you handled yourself very well on the radio. Bryce also told me about how well you did earlier at the ravine." Manning stopped and looked her directly in the eye. "I remember when that scenario first got dropped on me and I didn't do nearly so well. What I'm trying to say is that you've made remarkable progress in your training. Bryce suggested, and I agreed, that we give you an 'in-county certification,' effective immediately."

"What's that mean?" Katie asked, her fear turning to a bit of excitement at his words.

"It means you and Magnum are considered mission-ready for searches in Kitsap County only," Manning told her. "You won't get to go on every search—some assignments will still be too advanced for you. And you still have to pass a full certification test before we let you go outside the county."

Katie had been near tears when the conversation started, and the relief of not being in trouble opened the floodgates. "This is legal?" she managed to ask between sobs.

"Totally. And we're not doing this as some kind of favor. There's actually a reason," Manning continued. "We're issuing you a 'license to learn' by letting you respond to some carefully chosen searches, with your experience level in mind."

"Thank you…thank you," Katie managed to blurt out, shaking Manning's hand with both of hers, like a water pump. And while she was usually unfailingly polite, she had only one thing on her mind. "I gotta go tell Bryce…"

"Um, he knows," Manning's voice trailed off as Katie bolted. "It was his idea…"

Bryce turned as he heard someone running toward him, and was almost knocked over as Katie enveloped him in a hug.

"Hey…we're at a mission…can't do that now, you know." Someone had died, and the deceased person's family might not appreciate a celebration.

"Bryce, did you hear? They're going to…oh, right…you were in on it." It was all starting to sink in. She unwound her arms from Bryce's shoulders.

"Yes, I know," Bryce replied. "And it's not just because I love you. You earned the next step, and I hope Gary explained that it's a teeny baby step. Some searches, not all, and nothing outside our county."

"Yes, yes, I get it," was Katie's response. "But to think, we're going on actual missions!"

"It's gonna be great," Bryce said. "I'll miss having you as my field support, but you really have earned this. And you already have your first find, so that ticket is punched."

"We have," Katie said. "Oh…I gotta go tell Magnum."

Bryce understood the desire to give good news to one's dog. He'd done precisely the same thing when he and Sierra were first certified.

Chapter Four
Up a Tree

It was an unusual night for a search—the kind of weather in which people seldom go missing. The sky was moonlit, there were no clouds, and only a gentle breeze blowing in from the south. But an hour or so earlier, a woman had called 9-1-1 to report her boyfriend and his buddy didn't return from what should have been a short hike at a local tree farm.

SAR teams were gathering at a nearby county-owned maintenance shed to get ready, with Gary Manning in the role of Operations Chief.

"At least it's a good one for Katie and Magnum to start their careers," Manning told Bryce. "Nice terrain, a relatively small area, and yeah…a pretty straightforward search."

"Actually, I'm a feeling a little déjà vu," Bryce said. "The last time I was in this neighborhood looking for two missing dudes, and they were 'duuuudes,' it turned out they'd gotten high and fallen asleep under a tree."

"I remember that one," Manning replied. "Wasn't the girlfriend all whizzed off…it was like the three month anniversary of their first date or something? Mr. Pothead zoned out on what would probably have been a pretty decent evening."

The two shared a short laugh, and then Bryce went back to his original concern. "Gary, this really doesn't make sense. Two guys, lost in a relatively small tree farm, reported missing by a girlfriend. The place is covered with logging roads that all head down to the highway. There's just no reason for anybody to stay lost here."

"What you're saying is that I should probably make sure the good Detective Hicks has told us the whole story," Manning replied.

Bryce looked at him. "It's a crappy job, but somebody's gotta do it."

Of all the deputies who led searches, Detective Waylon Hicks was everybody's least favorite. Bryce didn't know it, but Hicks was a disappointment to most of the Sheriff's Office as well. He became a legend his first night out of the academy by forgetting to bring his gun to work. For most of a decade he'd performed just well enough to avoid being fired. His fellow detectives joked that their biggest unsolved mystery was how he could ever have been promoted into their ranks.

Bryce continued to get Sierra and all his equipment ready for the search. The two of them would be going out without a support person, something Bryce didn't like to do at night. If he fell and hit his head, the thumb-less Sierra would be unable to call for help. But it was occasionally done, especially if the unit was short of searchers.

Just as Bryce was about to leave the command post, he saw Manning coming back with a big smile on his face.

"You called it, brother," Manning said. "Hicks confirms the two guys we're looking for have a history of drug use."

"Annnd?"

"And what? They're dopers." Manning seemed annoyed at Bryce for pushing the issue.

"Whaddaya mean 'and what?'" Bryce added some annoyance of his own. "It would be really helpful to know their drug of choice. Are we gonna be finding a couple of sleepy stoners, heroin addicts who needs Narcan, or a pair of crackheads beating on their chests?"

"OK, I'll go ask," Manning said with a tone of resignation. When he returned, his eyes were bigger than Bryce had ever seen them.

"Meth," Manning blurted out. "He's asking us to go look for a couple of meth addicts. With histories of paranoia."

Hicks was really living up to his reputation that night. That was basic safety information which should have been shared with all searchers.

Bryce took a stand. "I'm not going out alone, that's for sure. And neither is Katie. We'll have to double up and she'll go as my support."

"That's going to break her heart," Manning said. "She was pretty excited about her first search."

"I know," Bryce said. "But we were clear that she isn't ready for all missions at this point. I don't think she's ready to deal with a pair of paranoid meth users alone. For that matter, I'm not either."

Bryce hurried over to Katie and filled her in. As he spoke, her shoulders slumped.

"Can't you find somebody else to go as my support?" she pressed. "Give me some big guy or something?"

"We don't have the people," Bryce replied softly. "I'm sorry. You'll have to put Magnum in the car and come as my support."

"I know," Katie sighed, acquiescing. "It's head vs. heart. My heart was set on this, but my head knows you're right." She put Magnum back in her car and nuzzled his head. "Sorry, buddy. Next time."

The two headed over to Bryce's Suburban. Their assignment was to search a patch of woods just outside the tree farm in case the men had lost their bearings and wandered out.

About ten minutes into the woods, Bryce knew they weren't going to find anybody there. The terrain was steep and slippery, and covered with an especially nasty form of brush called devil's club. When touched, the thorns break off under your skin so tweezers are useless at getting them out. Not even someone in a drug induced haze would plow uphill through devil's club on muddy ground. The assignment was a loser, but they'd complete it.

The priority in search and rescue is finding the person. Second best is determining where the person *isn't*. Bryce, Sierra and Katie spent nearly two hours becoming very satisfied that the two missing men weren't in their assigned search area.

"Base, 44," Bryce called.

"44, this is Base. Go ahead."

"44...we've finished this assignment. Nothing seen, no interest by the dog, and it's ugly here. Unlikely that anybody would choose this over the easier brush back in the tree farm."

"Roger that, 44. We'll focus on the tree farm then. Can you cover a couple of roads over there?"

"Sure. Let me check Sierra for thorns but assuming there's nothing in her feet or eyes we'll head over."

* * *

It was a short drive back to the tree farm, and Bryce was surprised to find Hicks at the gate.

"One down, one to go," was his comment. "One walked out and we've got him."

"Great," Bryce replied. "Any info on where his buddy might be?"

"Well, that's the problem. This guy's story, and the story from the girlfriend, aren't matching. With meth, you never know. We could be looking for a body."

Bryce again replied with "great," but it was exaggerated and with a sarcastic inflection. "I'll still handle this like a live search, and count on Sierra to tell me if the news is different. Where do you want us to check?"

"There's a buncha roads in the west end of the farm. Just check those and see what you find." Hicks replied.

Bryce held out his map, hoping that Hicks would at least mark the roads or area he wanted covered. Hicks' pen never left its pocket.

"Use your judgement," Hicks said, waving at the map. "Kinda over here, kinda over there." The man couldn't even be bothered to think up a specific assignment. "No need to crush brush, just walk these roads and see if the dog gives you anything."

"Okay," Bryce said, trying to sound cheerful when he wasn't. "We'll just poke around and see who's out there. Any reason to think this guy will be violent when we find him?"

"His friend admits the meth use, but says he's pretty mellow despite," Hicks said. "You'll be fine."

"No worries," Bryce said, turning away from Hicks. "Hey...Katie...you ready to head out?"

Katie stuffed the wrapper from an energy bar in her pocket and pulled her pack on. "Yup, you lead I'll follow."

The trio checked the first logging road and numerous side trails with no response. Sierra was very good about checking side trails and returning if no scent was present. Bryce could wait at the main road, and head out on a trail only if Sierra didn't return right away. It made for very efficient searching.

On the second road, Bryce noticed saw Sierra looking to her right, but she didn't leave the road. The area was relatively clear of underbrush and it was unusual for Sierra not to follow up on the slightest whiff of scent.

"Is that a deer?" Katie asked, squinting. In the dim moonlight filtering through the tree cover, Bryce could finally see the outline of a deer. It was hard to spot, and if Katie hadn't said something Bryce would likely have missed it.

"Looks like it." Bryce said. "'Splains why she's just looking there and not following up."

"I don't know you got her so focused," Katie exclaimed. "I'm pretty sure Magnum would have been over there like a rocket. Sierra's not even moving."

"It's why we make the reward such a party." Bryce said. "You make finding humans a big enough deal, deer just don't measure up. Magnum'll figure it out."

Sierra, having apparently satisfied herself that the smell was not one which would lead to "ball time," trotted on down the road.

Bryce and Katie followed, until the woods gave way to a clear cut, an area that had been logged and was now ready for replanting. Sierra had little interest in heading off that way, but the two humans, obviously taller than Sierra, could see a light.

"Think that's him?" Katie asked.

"I doubt it. At night, lights miles away can seem much closer. They're temping, but Sierra's not showing any interest."

"How about if I check it out?" Katie asked.

"No, stay with me," Bryce was firm. "Even if it is him, I don't want you making contact alone. If we don't find him elsewhere we'll come back here later."

The three of them continued down the road, but the further they went, the further Sierra got from Bryce. Her trot became a run, and she was soon out of sight around a corner.

"Let's try to keep up," Bryce said. "Looks like she's onto something."

Bryce hurried to catch up with Sierra, who had come to the end of the logging road and was moving through thick brush at top speed. Bryce followed as quickly as was safe. Soon Sierra's bell was out of earshot, and Bryce had to rely on her GPS collar to know where she was.

His hand-held display put her in some trees about halfway down a ravine. It showed she had made several circles around one spot, and was now heading back toward Bryce.

"I'm over here," he hollered, making the job of finding him easier for Sierra. She arrived, skidded into a full-stop sit, and had her eyes locked on Bryce's.

"Show me!" was Bryce's response, and his dog was gone. Bryce and Katie followed as quickly as the terrain allowed, but the GPS showed Sierra had returned to the same spot. When they caught up, she was still going in circles, looking up. Bryce followed her eyes with his light, and the mystery was solved.

"Hey, bud, what the heck are you doing up in a tree at 2am?" Bryce asked, trying to deliberately sound confused. He didn't want to trigger an argument with someone who might already be paranoid.

"Just hanging out," came the reply.

"Okay…we're from Search and Rescue. Are you Bill? Your friends called us." Bryce didn't say Bill's friends had called the police. He'd skip that part, at least for now.

"You sure you're from Search and Rescue?" Bill asked. "How do I know that?"

Alarm bells were starting to go off in Bryce's head. The guy was paranoid, and at least wondering about Bryce and Katie's true identity.

"Well, we found you here in the middle of the woods, didn't we?" Bryce replied, also in the lightest possible tone. "Your buddies admitted you occasionally do a little meth. Could that be what's making you afraid of us?" He wasn't sure the approach would work, but tackling a problem head-on has its advantages.

"Yeah, that's why I'm out here. When I get like this I just get away from everybody so I don't go off on them."

Bryce lowered his voice and adopted a serious tone. "Well, I gotta respect how you're handling things. Up a tree at 2am is a little odd, but at least you're not beating on somebody."

"Or trying to run them down."

"Say again?" Bryce asked.

"I just thought you might be that guy. He's probably going to try and kill me…you know…no witnesses."

"Witnesses to what?" Bryce asked. He was starting to connect some dots.

"Never mind…I shouldn't have said anything."

"Somebody tried to get you to run somebody down?" Bryce had no business pushing the issue, but he had an advantage: he wasn't the cops. People tell searchers things they never tell police, and Bryce was going with it.

"Look, I'm a doper but I'm not a murderer. I'll lie, cheat and sure as hell steal to get my drugs. But I'm not killing anybody…except myself maybe."

"Well, there's help for that, you know," Bryce offered. "Why don't you come down and let's talk? I'm getting a sore neck looking up at you."

"I'm staying right here," Bill-in-the-tree replied. "If he asked me to murder somebody then he might ask *you* to murder *me*. I'll stay up here, thank you. You're not gonna call the cops, are you?"

Bryce decided to go head-on again. "I'll be honest with you, my friend. The police are a part of every search we do, and I'll have to let them know Sierra found you."

"Screw you! You're gonna dime me out and I'll be kicking in jail."

"I'm not so sure. Sitting in a tree at 2am is a little weird, but it's not a crime. The landowner doesn't care you're out here, so you're not trespassing. Do you have warrants?" Bryce asked. If the answer were yes, Bryce would be even less happy with Hicks. SAR teams don't chase criminals.

"I don't think so. I made all my court dates," was the reply from above.

"Okay, let's do this. I'll get my team to let your friends know you're okay. That's the big issue. We'll have to tell the detective we found you, but I really wish you'd talk to him about this killing thing. If somebody asked you to kill somebody, that's a big deal."

"Nope....never should have said anything. If you say I did, I'll call you a liar." Bill had forgotten that Katie was a few yards away, and heard everything.

"Let me call this in to base, and you think for a while. I'll be back with ya," Bryce said, stepping away from the tree.

"Base, Dog 44," was the radio call.

"Dog 44, Base. Go ahead."

"This is Dog 44…we've located Bill. He's just fine and where he wants to be right now. But I'm thinking a detective might want to toddle out here and talk to him." Bryce passed the coordinates, with directions from the logging road.

"I'll check with the detective. Stand by…"

"44, standing by." Bryce stayed away from Bill, so he wouldn't hear whatever came back over the radio.

"44, Base. The detective says he has no reason to talk to Bill if he's okay and not the victim of some crime. He says mark the location in your GPS and come on back."

Bryce didn't like it, but wasn't surprised. Hicks was at his sloppy best. He'd try and talk to him when they got back to base.

"Base, 44 copies. We're en route back without the subject."

* * *

The walk to the trailhead, and the drive back to base, took about 30 minutes. Bryce tried to steel himself for the difficult conversation to come.

"Hey, Detective Hicks, can we talk for a moment?"

"Yeah…whaddaya need?" he replied. Hicks clearly didn't want to talk, but couldn't come up with an excuse quickly enough.

"I talked with Lenora a couple weeks back…"

Hicks interrupted before Bryce could continue. "That's Detective Hogan to you."

"Yes, sir. I spoke to Detective Hogan and she's got a hit and run that maybe was deliberate…"

Interrupted again. "What's that got to do with some meth-head up a tree?"

Bryce wanted to tell Hicks to just listen for a change, but that wouldn't have worked.

"Bill-the-Meth-Head said something about being approached and asked to run some guy down. In his paranoid state, he thought the fellow who tried to hire him was now trying to kill him to...."

Hicks interrupted a third time, this time raising his voice. Katie and most of the other searchers could hear him.

"Listen kid," Hicks snarled. "Just because you got lucky on that Chimera thing doesn't mean you get to come in here and start solving our cases for us. Your job is to find missing people and it ends there, understand?"

"Yes, sir." Bryce decided he'd be the adult in the conversation, and not argue in front of everyone. "Your call, just letting you know." That was as insubordinate as Bryce would be in the field.

"I heard it too," came a voice from behind him. It sounded like Katie, but in a tone Bryce hadn't ever heard. He turned to see her walking toward them, her eyes fixed on Hicks. "The man clearly said he'd been asked to kill someone. He wasn't rambling."

"Katie, it's okay." Bryce tried calming her down. She looked right over his shoulder at Hicks.

"You need to listen when people tell you stuff," she continued. "I was there. I heard what he said, and I believe him."

"You better get her under control, mister," Hicks retorted, now in full-throated anger. "I know they gave her some kinda special dispensation to search, but if she ever says something like that again it'll be her last search."

"Talk to me," Katie said, still fixated on Hicks. "You don't need to talk through my boyfriend, he's not my protector…"

"Katie…stop it," Bryce continued.

Finally, Katie moved her gaze from Hicks to Bryce. "He had no business talking to you that way."

"It's okay," Bryce said. "He's just a little more blunt than the other detectives. We can deal with it."

Hicks continued his rage. "You two haven't even begun to see how blunt I can be. You can both expect a call from Bob Wright, and if he takes my advice you'll both be out of SAR."

"Dial it down, detective." Gary Manning had heard the commotion, and felt compelled to intervene. He'd been in SAR longer than Hicks had been with the department.

"I don't know what started all this," Manning began. "But it ends now. You will not talk to volunteers that way. If you even think about screwing with Bryce and Katie I'll quit SAR. I suspect most of our members will follow. I guarantee we'll make sure the Sheriff knows you're the reason."

The color drained from Hicks' face, and he took a step backwards. "Okay, I'm sorry. But these kids can't come back here telling me how to run my case."

Manning took a step forward. "Somebody *better* tell you how to run your case. You almost sent unarmed volunteers out alone after paranoid meth addicts. That better never happen again or it's another conversation I'll be having with the Sheriff."

"Awright, awright," Hicks muttered. "Forget I said anything. The guy's been found, case closed. Let's all go home." Hicks got in his car and left.

The man in the tree would get the peace and quiet he was seeking. At least for the moment.

Chapter Five
Too Many Bodies

"The coroner's goin' broke...that's how many bodies there are. Tell me that's just an accident."

Detective Sgt. Bob Wright was frustrated. He was tolerant of pushback from his subordinates, but Hicks was jumping up and down on his last nerve. Hicks routinely put more effort into avoiding work than it would take to simply *do* the work.

"Stuff happens," Hicks argued. "And sometimes it happens in cycles. We go a while with no deaths, and then we get a bunch. It doesn't mean somebody's out there killing people."

The argument was an old one—but this time the trigger for concern was a little different. In Kitsap County, the coroner is elected, and is not necessarily a doctor. Autopsies are done under contract by board-certified forensic pathologists. The more syllables in your title, the bigger your fee.

"Not only are autopsies themselves busting his budget, but last month he had to rent space in two mortuaries because his freezer was full." retorted Wright. "That's more than just an upswing or a 'cycle.'"

As a manager, Wright could have simply given an order. But as a leader, he'd found that getting his people on board generally got better results. To that end, he tolerated difficult conversations. Sometimes people came around, and if not they at least felt heard.

"Maybe folks are getting more clumsy…or stupid." Hicks replied, starting to get even louder. "They're finding ever-new ways to kill themselves. It doesn't mean we have to get involved."

Instead of raising his voice, Wright lowered his tone. That would force Hicks to listen closely just to hear. "I think we should be involved. Even if we don't see evidence of homicide in any single case, when we take them as a group we might find something. I'd like you to go back over every one of these supposedly accidental deaths and see if there are any common threads between them."

"And just when am I going to find time to do that?" Hicks was too dumb to realize he was shooting himself in the foot. "We're so busy processing scenes I don't have time to go huntin' for clues on what are obviously accidental deaths."

"If you're that busy processing scenes, it kinda makes my point, doesn't it?" Wright finally moved back to a more boss-like tone of voice. "For this last bunch of deaths, and any new ones, work 'em up like they were all homicides. I don't care if the next guy gets hit by lightning. I wanna know who'd have reason to pray for a thunderstorm."

Hicks reloaded, and shot himself in the other foot. "What about heart attacks…? Y'know there are poisons that mimic that."

"Great idea!" Wright responded, trying his best to sound positive. "There are probably some routine hospital deaths that we haven't even been told about. Those will give us a bigger pool to check for commonalities."

"I didn't mean…" Hicks' voice trailed off.

Wright gave him a look that signaled the conversation was over. "I know you 'didn't mean,' but I do. I want to hear by Friday that you've at least reached out to the coroner and gotten him started on a list. Do a spreadsheet. Figure out some categories we might not usually check out. Hobbies, side jobs, favorite sports, go crazy. If these are homicides, there's gotta be one thing that connects them."

As Hicks stormed out, Wright put his head in his hands. He was well aware that his substandard detective would drag his feet, claim he was overworked, and find anything else to do besides follow directions. Wright had seen it from Hicks before, but this time he'd document everything. If Hicks came through, maybe they'd catch a killer. If he did a poor job, he'd have the evidence he needed to bounce his butt back to patrol. Wright didn't like setting somebody up for failure, but Hicks was a special case, and getting more special all the time.

"Is this a good time?" In his doorway was Lenora Hogan, who'd been working the hit-and-run case.

"Always, for you." Wright replied, grateful to have a professional detective in his presence. "Something up?"

"Well, yeah, but no surprise. The blood from the fender of that car matched our victim. It's definitely the hit and run vehicle," Hogan said.

"I've got Hicks looking into whether it's really a hit and run. You okay with him messing around in your case?" Wright was the kind of boss who routinely asked subordinates if a plan would work for them.

"If he runs true to form, he won't be in my way," Hogan replied with a smile. "Oops, was that my outside voice?"

"Tell you what. I'll play the kindly boss and tell him he doesn't need to work up that one case. The prospect of less work will please him. But I still want you to do the work-up, and share everything with him."

"That's fine. I'm pretty much done with it anyway," Hicks replied. "The whole mystery of the car smacks of a murder, but I can't find anything about the victim to make him a target. He doesn't have any girlfriends. His wife doesn't have any boyfriends. It can't be drugs, there's barely an aspirin in the house."

"You searched the house?" Wright interrupted. "How do you know about aspirin?"

"The wife gave us consent," Hogan said. "Once she heard it might have been deliberate she opened up everything. Poor woman will probably lose the house without her husband's income. Not even enough insurance to cover the mortgage."

Wright trusted Hogan's instincts. "That means we can probably rule her out as a suspect. But we need to cross-reference your info with all our other supposedly-accidental deaths. Since this one likely IS murder, let's call it Case Zero. Everything else gets tested against this case. Tell me about the car again."

Hogan could recite the car's history from memory, almost down to the multiple VIN numbers stamped on the various parts that had clearly come from different cars.

"It was an insurance total. Several totals, actually," she said. "The engine is from one car, the transmission from another, the rear end from a third. The person got ahold of at least three identical models of the same car, all of which had been in major collisions and crossed off the books over at Motor Vehicles."

Rebuilding wrecks was a perfectly legal cottage industry in Washington. Junkmeisters could buy cars that insurance companies had decided weren't worth repairing, and repair them. They could sell them for a modest profit if they left off a few of the more expensive amenities. Rebuilt wrecks frequently didn't have air bags or ABS systems. Crumple zones might not crumple correctly. As a rookie cop, Wright had investigated one rebuilt wreck in which the seat belts were attached to the floor with tiny screws.

"But then the guy comes up with a completely false ID for the registration?" Wright asked.

"Correct," was the reply from Hogan. "The name is false, the registered address comes up in the middle of a lake…this car is as cold as you can get. And he registered it at a licensing office that doesn't have surveillance video. How would he ever know that?"

"Wow. If not for the other deaths, I'd think CIA…" Wright's voice trailed off at the end.

"CIA? Seriously?" Hogan was intrigued.

"A few years back a couple of reporters figured out that our Motor Vehicle Department was happy to give the CIA false IDs, false papers on cars, just like they give our narcs," Wright explained. "It became kind of an international incident. Any spy, anywhere in the world, using Washington ID was in danger of being outed."

"Righto" was Hogan's reply on her way out the door. "Want me to tell Hicks he's off the hook for this one?"

"No...send him in on your way out. Just once I'd like to get a smile out of him."

* * *

"You won't need to work up Hogan's car case," Wright told Hicks. "She's far enough down the road that we'll let her finish it."

"Oh, the little lady doesn't want me messing in her case...is that it?" Hicks' ego was winning out over his dedication to sloth.

"Aw jeez, does nothing make you happy?" Wright pleaded. "I told you she's already done most of the casework. She'll share everything with you, and if she misses something it'll give you a chance to gloat. Let it go."

Hicks went back to his desk, still mulling over the best way to avoid this particular bit of busywork. The boss wanted a spreadsheet, so he'd give him a spreadsheet. He just needed some categories across the top. Or maybe he'd put the victims across the top, and categories down the side.

The list was uninspired.

- Employment Type
- Marital Status
- Cheating on Spouse?
- Gambling?
- Religion
- Personal Investments
- Homeowner vs Renter
- Insurance

- Types of Cars Owned
- Hobbies
- Activity at Death
- Natural or Accidental?
- Drug Use?
- Drinking Habits (location, type)

"That oughtta keep him happy," Hicks thought. He booted up his spreadsheet program and started filling in the categories. He decided to put habits down the side, and run victims across the top. That way any patterns would show up as a line from left to right. Now he just needed to put the victims' names across the top.

"Hey, Bill," he said into the phone. "It's Hicks over at the S.O. Got a minute?"

Bill Devers was the number-two man in the county coroner's office. Hicks preferred dealing with him because he wasn't elected. The man been with the office nearly 30 years, and his energy level had declined since his young go-getter days. He was Hicks' kinda guy.

"Sure, what's up?" Devers asked.

"Oh, the boss has me runnin' some stuff down. A waste of time, mostly," Hicks almost whispered. "I need to look for patterns in all these accidental deaths. He thinks they're not accidental."

"What!? That's ridiculous," Devers replied.

"I know, but he's the boss. Like I've got time to fool around with this." The conspiratorial tone continued. "Get this—he even wants me checking hospital deaths, which is why I'm calling."

"Dunno that I can give you those," Devers replied. "HIPAA and all. Those folks died under competent medical care and we can't just spread the details around everywhere."

Hicks was lazy, but that wasn't his biggest fault. Pride held that place of honor. He was a cop...a detective...and he was used to getting what he asked for. Despite his desire to avoid hard work, that pride led him to demand the information.

"Hey, I'm in the club. This is an official investigation. I don't like it any more than you do, but this is the Sheriff's Office asking."

"Sorry, man," Devers said in the tone of someone who's digging in their heels. "Routine hospital deaths are not within the purview of the Sheriff's Office and I'm not going to federal prison for leaking information."

Hicks began to raise his voice. "You are way out of line...*man*. I've got orders to check out every death in the last three months and I'm not going in front of Internal Affairs to explain why it didn't happen. I'm just looking for names and cause of death. I can get it through a public records request if I need to."

"No ya can't," was Devers' reply. "Medical records and death certificates are confidential. The public can't get them and you can't get them. I'll tell you anything you want to know about bodies your office found, or that were handled as suspicious deaths. We obviously work together on those. But we're not...you're not...digging into the private medical records of people who died natural deaths."

"I'll get a warrant," Hicks replied, not mentioning that during his stellar career as a detective he'd never actually written a search warrant. As a result, Devers knew the law better than Hicks.

"Search warrants don't work for fishing expeditions. You have to convince the judge that a crime's been committed and evidence will be found at the place you're searching. There's not a judge on the planet who will issue a warrant just to figure out if there's a crime at all."

Devers was right, and Hicks was stumped. He wasn't sure how to handle Devers' intransigence, and he wasn't sure how he'd explain his failure to Wright.

"Okay, how about if we try this? You just give me their names and dates of birth," Hicks pleaded. "You don't need to give me their medical records. I'm just looking for commonalities in their lives. If I've got enough information to positively ID them, I can do the rest without getting into their medical files."

"Right," came Devers' reply. "You're just gonna call the widow Jones, say you're from the Sheriff's Office, and ask HER a bunch of questions about…what? 'Did your husband have any bad habits that might have gotten him murdered?'"

"That's for me to worry about," Hicks said. "What I need from you are the names, and there's gonna be a big stink between our offices if I don't get them."

Devers remained unimpressed. "Go ahead, run to the Sheriff. He can work it out with my boss, and I'm betting my guy tells your guy to stuff it."

Hicks slammed the phone down without even saying goodbye. He knew that would get him a rude conduct complaint if Devers said anything, but in this context he'd take it. It would at least look like he was fighting for what his boss wanted. He walked down the hall to Wright's office.

"Hey, Bob, got a minute?" Hicks asked deferentially. "I'm already stuck on something and maybe you can help me figure it out."

Wright figured that "stuck on something" was code for trying to get out of work. He ended up being surprised at what Detective Hicks said next.

"I know I didn't want to check all those deaths," he explained, "but now I've kinda got my dander up. You'll probably have to write me up for hanging up on the guy but I really want to get this information."

"If slamming down the phone kept you from saying something worse, then maybe it was the better part of valor," Wright replied. "If he beefs I'll have to make it official, but until then let's just consider this verbal counseling."

"Thanks, but now how do we go on and get the data you want?"

"Thought about the newspaper?" Wright asked.

"Huh?"

"The newspaper," Wright explained. "You know, that thing you never read? Behind the obituaries there's a section for legal notices, which are required as part of probate. All the deaths are there."

Hicks was incredulous. "Then why did Devers give me such a hard time? I mean…if it's in the paper anyway?"

"It's a legal notice, done by executors as part of probate," Wright said. "It's to make sure debtors get their bills turned in. There's nothing medical about it, so it probably wasn't on his radar any more than yours."

"Now I just have to find a bunch of old newspapers, I guess," Hicks said.

"Hope you've got a library card."

Chapter Six

Train Wreck

Alan Reeves didn't keep the neatest office in the world, but he'd never seen anything as bad as this. It was almost like his predecessor had deliberately tried to make things confusing.

Reeves had done his due diligence before buying the insurance brokerage. He'd looked at bank records. He'd looked at investments. He'd looked at filings with regulators, customer lists and monthly bills. What he hadn't looked at was the office itself—a huge mistake.

At least now he knew why the previous owner always wanted to meet off-site. The excuse had been so that the brokerage's two employees wouldn't know the firm was for sale. Once Reeves got the keys, it was clear the guy hadn't wanted a potential buyer to see his mess.

"Filing by piling," Reeves muttered to himself. He'd fired employees for that kind of sloppy work. "How much could a few file cabinets have cost?"

The good news was that the brokerage had been well-capitalized and was clearly profitable. The bank records were indisputable and in the two weeks he'd owned the place, his bank balance had grown by the expected amount.

What Reeves couldn't figure out was *how* the place turned a profit. He'd heard the phrase "follow the money," and couldn't. There was no way to trace a bill paid by a customer to a few dollars of commission in his own pocket. God help him if anybody ever complained to the insurance commissioner. He'd never be able to explain things to an auditor.

"Melissa, could you come in here please?" Reeves called to the next room.

Melissa Fisher was the only remaining employee of the firm. Bonnie Shelton had been the office secretary since before Melissa was born, but had retired when Reeves bought the business.

"Quite the mess, eh?" Fisher observed. "I saw it for the first time after Bonnie retired. I almost quit."

"What do you mean you 'saw it for the first time?'"

"I was always told to stay out of the file room," Fisher explained. "These records are confidential and privacy was a big deal, what with federal rules and all. I'd be happy to try and clean things up for you."

"Right now I kinda hate to mess with it," Reeves responded. "It sounds like we're both pretty clueless. You think Bonnie would come out of retirement?"

"I doubt that," Melissa said. "She all but tossed a match over her shoulder when she strolled out. She was never coming back. That's why I was thinking I'd take a shot."

Reeves had other ideas, though he'd been Melissa's boss just long enough to know she'd be unhappy.

"What you can do," he requested, "is keep these piles from getting any deeper. Worst case all these policies will renew over the next year and we'll have fresh paperwork. A year from now we can follow Bonnie's lead and burn this stuff if we want. So go order a couple file cabinets and let's get a decent system going forward. Nothing new makes its way into this room."

"Got it," Fisher responded. "Though I'd still like a shot at cleaning this up."

Reeves thought for a moment; then said, "Let me take a run at re-hiring Bonnie first. If we can get her back, it'll be faster for everyone. If not, then you and I will have a go."

Melissa turned and headed back for her desk. "Okay," she sighed. "Just like before, I'm being told to stay out of that room."

Reeves didn't have time to analyze her unhappiness. Instead, he turned to his own desk and picked up the phone.

"Hey, what kind of piece of crap did you sell me?" he asked.

The voice on the other end was immediately defensive. "I sold you a profitable firm. What's your problem?"

"My problem," Reeves responded, "is that I can't figure out *how* it's profitable. "Your records are in such bad shape I can't tell which end is up."

"You're right, they were. I'm probably too nice a guy." Suddenly the voice was trying to sound kind, and smooth. Insurance salesmen are good at that. "You met Bonnie, right? My old secretary? Well, in her later years she got a little sloppy. I knew she'd be retiring soon and I didn't have the heart to bust her chops."

"Um, no. I'm not buying that." Reeves was starting to get worked up. "You didn't even have file cabinets in your filing room. How was Bonnie or anybody supposed to set up a filing system without file cabinets?"

"Look, it's your firm now and if you don't know how to run one that's not my problem," the salesman responded, a bit less kindly. "These kinds of phone calls are exactly why I retired."

"Okay," Reeves said. "I get that. But can you tell me if there's any reason to the riddle? Term life on one side, whole life on the other? Car insurance in the middle? I mean, nothing's alphabetical…nothing's in order of policy number…just give me a clue."

"It's your firm now and anything I would do would amount to meddling. You bought it and you own it. End of story."

Reeves couldn't believe his ears. The guy had seemed like kindest, most helpful man in the world. But that apparently only lasted until the check cleared.

Reeves tried dangling money. "I wouldn't mind bringing you back as a consultant," he offered. "Then you'd be on my payroll and there'd be no question of meddling."

"Haha, gotta go," was the reply. "It's happy hour down at the bar…and it's ladies night. I'm buying drinks with *your* money."

<Click>

"Wow," was all Reeves could think. Apparently the concept of service after the sale was not in play here. He'd have to see if

Bonnie Shelton could sort things out, or he and Melissa would have to waste most of a week sorting through piles.

It was not, he thought, how the owner of a business should be spending their time.

Chapter Seven
Siddown, You're Rockin' the Boat

"You have one job," Bryce called out, over the sound of the outboard.

"I know," the boat driver yelled back. "Steer toward the dog's nose. If the dog looks in a particular direction, I'll steer that way."

"No, that's not what I'm looking for." Bryce moved closer so he wouldn't have to seem like he was yelling. "Your most important job is safety. If the dog goes overboard, and if we find anything she WILL try to go overboard, your only job is to kill the engine."

On water, Sierra was a bit schizophrenic in her search technique. Starting out, she'd be uncharacteristically zen-like. She'd quietly drape herself over the bow of their inflatable dinghy, put her nose almost to the water and then appear to go to sleep. Only the telltale flaring of her nostrils told Bryce she was awake and working as they went back and forth across the water.

That would all change dramatically if the odor of a drowning victim wafted to the surface. Bryce would suddenly find himself in the role of rodeo cowboy, trying to keep a bucking bronco from going overboard. He'd keep a tight hold on Sierra's floatation vest, and try to last the whole eight seconds.

"Roger on killin' the engine," the driver replied. "But do you still want me to steer toward her nose?"

"Yeah, sure," Bryce said. "If she just starts moving slowly down one side or the other, then bend it a little that way. It probably means she's curious about something, and we'll have go back and forth a couple times to get it nailed down."

The trio of Sierra, Bryce and the boat driver had been tasked with finding a male subject who'd jumped from a bridge upstream of the boat launch. His car had been found, abandoned and running, at the center of the bridge. Sierra wasn't expected to pinpoint the body's exact location. Her job was to narrow the area that divers would have to search in the traditional way, hand over hand in the inky blackness.

They got underway and started working into the current, toward the bridge, a distance of about a half-mile.

After only a few minutes of searching, Bryce realized he'd won the boat-driver lottery. Running the outboard motor with one hand, holding his GPS with the other, the driver was executing an almost perfect grid search despite both wind and current working against him.

Sierra remained her calm self for about 45 minutes. Then, almost imperceptibly, her head shifted slightly to the right. She wasn't yet pulling, or even drifting down the side of the boat. But Bryce caught the movement and so did his driver. Without prompting, the driver started a slow turn to the right, matching the subtle nature of Sierra's movement. "This guy IS good," Bryce thought.

The slow, sweeping u-turn back to the area of interest changed one important thing. Bryce had beed sitting on what was originally Sierra's left, holding the handle of her vest with his right hand. That was no problem when she detected odor to her right. Now, after a 270-degree turn, Bryce found himself between Sierra and the source of odor just as she got a real snootful. Sierra snapped her head to the left and tried crawling up Bryce's chest. Because she was going at him and not pulling away, he didn't have the leverage necessary to control her movements. She was about to take them both overboard.

"Sierra...gentle!" was Bryce's command, but Sierra was having none of it. The odor was there and for a golden retriever there's no downside to going in the water.

Then, unexpectedly, Bryce felt the burden of Sierra's weight on his chest lighten. Her paws were still flailing but he was no longer being forced backward out of the boat. Finally, he caught a glimpse of the boat driver using the handle on Sierra's floatation vest to control her...just a bit.

"Kill the engine," Bryce cried, uncharacteristically losing his cool. He didn't want any or all of them going overboard next to a spinning propeller.

"I popped it into neutral," was the calm reply. "I don't like shutting down completely in current like this. Now...you wanna throw that buoy before we drift too far away?"

Bryce reached down and tossed the orange marker just upstream of where Sierra had been looking. It was attached to a lead weight which would fall to the river bed and keep the buoy in place for divers. He grabbed the handle on Sierra's vest so the driver could get back to driving.

"Here you go girl! Nice job." Bryce offered Sierra her ball, which she promptly spit out before making another run at getting out of the boat.

"Pretty common reaction," Bryce told the driver. "On land, Sierra would kill for that ball. Not so much in a boat. We don't know why."

"I thought we were gonna lose both of you overboard. Looks like even the dive team could see what was going on."

Bryce looked back toward the boat launch, and the dry-suited drivers were already climbing into their boat. Bryce gave them a nod and a thumbs-up. They'd be at the buoy in a couple minutes and would "splash divers" in a couple more.

"Can we swing back right over the buoy?" Bryce asked. "I didn't get a chance to mark the location on my GPS."

"Gotcha covered," was the driver's response. "I marked it on mine while you were going all Friday-night-wrestling with Sierra."

"Wow, you're really taking good care of me. Thanks, man."

"No problem. I know our subject's in-laws, and I really want to get him back to them. Nobody had any idea he was suicidal."

"I never got the full story," Bryce said.

"Perfectly normal life. Wife, two kids, job, mortgage, car...then one night his car's parked at the middle of that bridge and he's not in it. The neighbors report hearing a splash, hence the call for boats and dogs."

"No mental health history?" Bryce's wheels were turning.

"Nothing. There's drugs that'll make you suicidal but he wasn't taking them. Plenty of money in the bank and his older kid just won an athletic scholarship so even college tuition wasn't an issue. There was nothing wrong in this guy's life."

"Well, suicide is a disease and we don't always know what's lurking in someone's brain," Bryce began, but his next thoughts were interrupted by the arrival of the dive boat.

"Which way from the buoy?" the team leader asked. Bryce knew they'd want to splash as close to the body as possible.

"I think we were pretty close," Bryce yelled back. "Maybe a little upstream from the buoy but not too far. Current will drag scent downstream, so I tossed it upstream from where Sierra was looking."

"Okay, thanks. You're welcome to stay in the neighborhood but please stand off with your propeller. Just enough oomph to counteract the current, if you don't mind."

"That'd be great," Bryce replied. "We'd like to watch."

And watch they did, for a whopping two minutes. One of the divers popped to the surface and had a short conversation with the topside leader. He gave a thumbs-up in Bryce's direction and headed back down.

"Found him already?" Bryce's driver asked. "Damn, that dog's good."

"You're no slouch as a boat driver either. I meant to tell you that was a nice grid you worked. Probably the best ride we've ever had."

"No worries, man. I'm from Louisiana and ran the bayous and crap growin' up as a kid. You start to mind-meld with the outboard after...hey, what's that?"

Bryce turned around to see the diver back at the side of his boat, and the team leader on his radio. Yet another boat was coming from the boat launch at high speed.

"That looks like the rescue divers...the ones they hold back in case the first team gets in trouble," Bryce's driver said.

"Well, something's up. Maybe we can...'HEY...WHAT'S UP?'" Bryce yelled toward the dive boat.

"Diver down...missing," the dive team leader yelled back. "Swing downriver a bit and see if you see anything. Just watch that damn propeller."

Louisiana bayou-man was smooth as silk maneuvering their small inflatable downstream of the dive boat. Bryce looked over the side for any sign of the missing diver, and noticed Sierra's nose was now over the side as well.

"Will the dog alert on a diver who's alive, or do they have to be..." the driver's voice trailed off.

"Are you kidding?" Bryce responded, eyes still focused on the water. "We train for water search using scuba divers. I don't know if it's the rubber suit or what...I only know that we were at the beach in Silverdale when a couple of divers walked out of the water. Sierra went as nuts as you saw her today."

"Well, whatever works," the driver yelled back. "I'm going to try and get ahead of the current, and see if he drifts down to us."

"Got him!" were the next words out of Bryce's mouth, followed by "Sierra, noooo!"

The ability to smell AND see their subject had put some extra energy in Sierra's alert. Bryce had been leaning over the side, just enough off-balance that Sierra could easily take him overboard. In a flash, they were both in the river.

Wiping the water from his eyes, Bryce could see the diver's lifeless body spread-eagle, face down, about five feet below the surface. He wasn't floating up, but wasn't sinking either. Bryce didn't know enough about diving to understand neutral buoyancy. He only knew the diver was lucky that someone could see him.

Bryce kept trying to reach down and grab the man, but his own vest kept him on the surface. The three divers from the other two boats were all searching underwater, and unaware of this discovery. With no help available, Bryce unclipped his own floatation vest, slipped it off, and went under.

The water had been cold to begin with, but when Bryce put his head under he got an instant brain freeze. It hurt so bad his eyes crossed, but he forced himself down. Depth was no issue—he'd been that far under water in his high school pool. His challenge was to overcome the crushing cold that after even just a few seconds was already making it difficult to move his arms.

Bryce pushed through the pain and managed to grab onto something on the man's scuba gear. He wasn't sure what, and prayed it was sturdy enough to hold the man's weight. Bryce then started kicking, bringing himself and his human cargo to the surface.

By that time the dive team leader had seen what was happening, recovered his men, and pulled up alongside Bryce's inflatable. The other divers grabbed their colleague from Bryce and tossed him in the rescue boat like they were playing water polo.

Climbing aboard, they immediately started CPR as both boats took off for the dock.

Sierra and Bryce were still in the water.

"Over here, man!" The boat driver was still covering Bryce's back. He held their emergency paddle by the wide end and offered Bryce the handle, helping him maneuver to the side of the boat as Sierra swam up alongside him.

"Get Sierra out," Bryce sputtered, even though he was so cold it was hard to talk. He managed to push on Sierra's butt while the driver grabbed her vest, and in short order, both were out of the water and all were headed to the launch.

"That was a seriously crappy move," the driver yelled. "You found their guy and they just roared off and left you."

"They knew you were right here," Bryce answered. "You got us out okay and look, they're already getting their guy in the medic unit. I get it."

"Well, I don't."

The rest of the trip in was made in silence.

* * *

"How's your guy?" Bryce asked the dive team leader. They'd at least called a second ambulance for Bryce, knowing he'd be dangerously cold. He was in the back compartment, being toweled off by firefighters and waiting to change clothes.

"His name's Bill Tarana, and he's not good," was the pained response. "His partner came up to say they'd found the guy who jumped. In fact, the lead weight on your buoy was between his legs. And then just that quick Bill was nowhere to be found."

"Damn, I'm sorry. I hope they're able to do something for him. Sometimes if the water's cold enough…"

"I'm really sorry we left you out there." The man interrupted, clearly shaken. "We were totally focused on Bill but we should have left one of our boats with you…"

Bryce jumped in to help the man save face. "I had a boat with me, and a really good driver. I'm just a little cold is all."

"You found our guy and we paid you back by abandoning you." The voice was moving from grief to anger. "Let me tell you that will NEVER happen again."

There was a knock at the door of the ambulance and through the window, a familiar face. Katie hadn't been able to respond when the original call went out. But she had turned on her SAR radio, only to pick up traffic about a diver down and a dog handler in the water.

"Are you okay? Were you in the water?" she asked, concern visible on her face.

"No, I took a short-cut through the sewer," Bryce responded, pointing to his soaking wet clothing. "Yes, I got in the water but it's no big deal. The guy was right there."

"Young lady, your boyfriend is a hero," the paramedic interjected. "I don't know if that diver will live, but the only reason he has any chance at all is thanks to Bryce."

In an instant, Katie went from afraid to angry. "Your job is to find people, not morph into some kind of lifeguard and jump in a river!"

"I didn't jump," Bryce replied, in the tone of a meek, chastized boyfriend. "Sierra pulled me overboard and the guy was right there. I just grabbed him is all."

"Slipped out of your life vest to grab him..." the paramedic interjected again.

"What!?" Katie's face flashed a look of anger that Bryce had never seen.

"Um, could we consider that private medical information, please?" Bryce asked the medic. "She didn't need to hear that."

"You were IN the river and took off your life vest? Do you know how cold it is this time of year?" Katie almost yelled. "Your lungs could have locked up and you'd have drowned too."

"Hon, it all worked out okay. Can we just think positive thoughts that the diver will come out of this?"

"Of course, but I'm also thinking of you." Katie was near tears. "You can't take risks like that. What was it they said in training? 'We don't trade rescuers for victims.'"

"I getcha, it just seemed like a good idea at the time. It's filed for future reference. Can you check on Sierra?" Bryce asked, doing a poor job of changing the subject. "I warmed up some chicken broth on my camp stove, but I want to make sure she's not still shivering."

With a final look that told Bryce he'd been caught, Katie left the ambulance to check on Sierra. Just as quickly another head popped in the door.

"How ya doin', bud?" Bob Wright didn't usually respond to suicides, but word of a diver down and Bryce in the water had changed the situation. It would also give him a chance to keep an eye on Hicks and make sure he treated even this obvious suicide as a murder.

"Starting to warm up, thanks. Katie's checking on Sierra."

"I walked by your truck," Wright replied. "She was sound asleep in her kennel. How'd you two end up in the water?"

"I was leaning over the side looking for the missing diver. When Sierra bolted she took me with her. Ah, geez…I just realized my radio's probably toast." The radio had been in Bryce's vest, and likely wouldn't react well to being dunked.

"We've got more," Wright replied gently. "I'm glad you're okay and thanks for finding that diver. Bill's a firefighter, you know. He held my hand a few years back while his buddies cut me out of my patrol car."

"Really?" It was a story Bryce had never heard.

"I was a rookie and being stupid. I was hotfooting it to back up a city officer and never quite made it to the scene. I wrapped my car around a utility pole. Is it true you took off your vest to go under?"

Bryce hung his head. "Katie's giving me hell over it."

"Well, the Sheriff'll probably give you a medal for heroism and then put a letter of reprimand in your file. You're lucky. I took a risk to help a fellow officer and damn near died. What if you'd both ended up floating face down in that water?"

"I know, but like I told Katie, it seemed like a good idea at the time…in the moment…I mean, I was there. You and Katie weren't."

"When I started in this biz we excused all kinds of reckless behavior in the name of heroism," Wright continued. "After a few losses we think differently now. Understand?"

"I guess so," Bryce acknowledged. "I doubt I'll ever have the chance to rescue another scuba diver, but I'll keep the general idea in mind."

"Good enough for me," Wright said, opening the door of the ambulance. "Looks like the city divers are here. They'll go retrieve the body for us—the fire guys are in no shape to dive anymore tonight. I'll put in a good word with the sheriff for ya."

"Thanks," Bryce said as the ambulance door swung shut. He didn't expect a parade for rescuing the diver, but he didn't want to be in trouble either.

* * *

The two men watched the dive boat approach the ramp, the victim's remains finally on board. As the boat throttled down, Wright was throttling up.

"Why aren't his hands bagged?" was Wright's question, watching the city divers' boat glide into the launch. Hicks was on board, doing his job in his usual half-baked fashion.

"I told you we treat all of these as homicides until proven otherwise," Wright added.

It was common for divers to have trouble getting recovered bodies into body bags, thanks to the effects of rigor mortis. For a period after death, the body stiffens in the position of death. If rigor is in effect, and the person died in an awkward position, they literally might not fit in a body bag. In this case, the dead man arrived at the dock partially bagged and covered with a tarp. A gust of wind revealed the unbagged hands to Wright.

"Aw, boss," Hicks began. "The guy jumped. I'll do the whole background thing like you want, but really? We're gonna bag hands and all that crap?"

"You're gonna bag hands and it's *not* crap." Wright was normally careful to correct employees in private, but not this night. "Tell me you photographed the bridge scene before they moved the car."

"It was just an abandoned car at the time," which was true and scored a minor point for Hicks. "I'll go back up and figure out where he went over."

Now Wright did lower his voice. "Better snap to, mister. I am serious as a heart attack that you are to take all unexplained deaths as homicides until you have three different ways of proving otherwise. You know what it takes to investigate a murder and if you want to remain a detective I'd better see you doing those things. Understand?"

"Got it," was Hicks' tight-jawed reply. But it was clear from the look on his face that he didn't "have it."

The two were interrupted by the deputy medical examiner bringing the deceased's personal belongings.

Wright gloved up and quickly scanned the items. He didn't trust Hicks to look them over with an open mind…maybe he wouldn't even look at them at all.

Wallet, car keys, pen from a shirt pocket and a cell phone case with a belt clip. Wright looked at the items from all sides and came back to the phone case. It was hard plastic, with a metal clip to hold it onto the owner's belt.

Hicks saw Wright beginning to focus on the case. "No phone, just the case. It probably popped out when he landed."

"You will ping the phone and make sure it made it to the center of the bridge," was Wright's response. "If it's in the water we'll probably never find it and that's okay. But we need to make sure that phone was with him when he jumped...if he jumped."

Hicks started to argue and stopped mid-word. "Right. Want me to fingerprint his car and all this stuff?"

"Yeah I do." Wright kept talking. "And what's this red stuff on the phone case? Same color as the bridge rail." The coroner's investigator was just pulling out, and Wright ran to flag him down.

"Hey...where on the body was this phone case?"

"Small of his back, oddly enough," he replied. "Carried it like some cops carry their off-duty guns, right above his butt crack."

Hicks never blinked. He showed no understanding of what the statement portended. Wright was dumbfounded at his detective's new level of cluelessness.

"Who climbs over a bridge rail backwards?" was the senior man's question. "You only go over backwards if you're pushed."

Chapter Eight

Murder as Murder

"Hey, man, this is really nice of you." Eddie Hartman had lost most of his friends, and he knew why. "I'm kinda hard to be nice to."

The benefactor who said, "Just call me Jake" had brought Hartman a good jacket, new shoes, and even a refurbished iPhone. He casually shrugged off Hartman's comment. "Well, sometimes I'm a jerk too…a big enough jerk to get thrown out of the Army." It was a lie, but lies came easy for the man who called himself Jake. Sometimes he lied when he didn't need to, just for the hell of it.

"You got kicked all-the-friggin-way out?! Man, that's something. What'd you do?" The hook was set. The homeless Hartman now saw the man bearing gifts as a kindred soul, a fellow bad-boy. Somebody he could join in hating the world.

Jake leaned in and winked. "Might've had something to do with a grenade simulator in the lieutenant's desk drawer." He'd never served, but had listened well when other men got to drinking.

"This L-T was always an ass. Now he's an ass who's deaf in one ear."

"Aw man, that's great," Hartman laughed. "I wish I coulda done something like that. My last boss didn't show me no respect, neither. I gave that company seven good months of my life and ended up with absolutely nothin' to show for it."

Actually, Hartman did have something to show for it, though he didn't know it. His former employer had been generous with benefits, and every employee got a $50,000 life insurance policy. Jake had handled the coverage and personally checked every application for "completeness." That meant finding potential victims. Hartman's app had dripped with opportunity. No family, his beneficiary a charity that served the homeless.

Jake rightly suspected Hartman wouldn't become a longtime employee. So when he left, Jake didn't pass along the company's instruction to cancel the policy. Instead, he changed the beneficiary and paid the continuing premium out of his own pocket. All Hartman had to do now was die. Somehow.

It had been no easy task disguising murders as accidental deaths. Jake couldn't repeat any scenario, lest the authorities notice a pattern. Running out of ideas, he'd decided the best way to hide this murder was to disguise it…as a murder.

As always, he needed intel on his planned victim. And there's no better way to get a homeless person to open up than by giving them free stuff. The phone, jacket and shoes loosened the tongue almost as well as booze. The only other thing needed was encouragement.

"Well, I think we can get you a job where you will get some respect," he said. "You're kind of the low hanging fruit around here." At the sound of that catchy phrase, Hartman's hard-to-like side came out immediately.

"I ain't no fruit, man. I mean, I got nothin' against gays or nothin', but I'm straight. Not that I can afford a girlfriend or anything right now."

"No, no, sorry," was Jake's response. "I didn't mean it that way. It's a just a saying…it means you're easy to help. Y'know, like an apple on a low branch is easy to pick." He looked at his protégé, leaned in and whispered. "You might have noticed there's a bunch of people around here that are really screwed up. They're gonna be living in tents till the day they die. You, on the other hand, have some potential. You can get out of this."

Hartman still didn't really get it, but the guy was bringing him clothes and a phone, so he wasn't going to argue. "I like girls, okay?" was his parting shot.

"Me too. Hey, who's that guy?" Jake asked, looking over Hartman's shoulder.

Even through the brush the old man's limp was hard to miss. They watched him make his way down the narrow, rutted trail, headed for his own little patch of homeless heaven.

"We just call him 'Gimp,' but he's a tough old bird," Hartman said. "Nobody knows his story, but nobody screws with him. Some younger guy saw the limp and assumed he'd be an easy mark. He was wrong. Word is that there's a sword built into that cane."

"Remind me to talk nicely to him," Jake said. "Looks like he's one-a those messed up dudes I was talking about."

"He's walking pretty good today," Hartman observed. "When he's really plastered he can barely get down that path, even with his cane."

"How often is he 'really plastered?'" was the obvious question.

"Most nights. Last summer there was a brush fire and I went over to wake him up. I shook him till it hurt and he never budged. All that alcohol in his system…if the fire had gotten to him he'd have gone up like a Roman candle."

Intel. *Great* intel. Jake realized his long-term plan for Eddie Hartman had just been adjusted. His motto was "Semper Gumby," which he liked to think was Latin for "always flexible."

"Okay, let's focus," Jake said returning to the main topic. "Be ready to answer that phone. I'll be calling in some favors to get you interviews."

"Will do. Can I use it for other stuff?" Hartman asked. Jake had a pretty good idea what "other stuff" meant, but he'd gone whole hog and gotten digital service too.

"Yup. You can surf all you want. Some employers will want you to fill out their apps online, so you can do it right from your phone. Whatever else you look at is no concern of mine."

"Cool!" was Hartman's response. He'd gotten kicked out of the library a couple times for viewing things other patrons didn't like seeing. This would solve his privacy problem. "But I gotta ask. How come you got me an iPhone and not one-a those pre-paid things over at the market?"

"It's about flash," Jake replied. "If you wanna *get* someplace, you gotta look like you're *goin'* someplace. A generic pre-paid phone says you're a homeless guy. An iPhone sends a message."

"What do I say if someone calls?"

"First, check your schedule," Jake said, drawing a quizzical look. "I know, you're available. But you want them to think you've got other stuff going on. So pretend to look at your date book. Ask them to move the interview by an hour one way or the other. But cave if they can't, and don't argue. If they push it just tell them you'll move the other appointment. "

"Okay…" Hartman said, not fully understanding.

"Then, wear the clean jacket and shoes I gave you. Show up and be respectful," Jake said. "Nobody gets offered a job as CEO right out of the gate. Just let them know you're a hard worker and willing to learn."

"Man, I know how to do a lot of stuff." Hartman started to prattle on. "I can fix things and paint stuff. And I'm a great carpenter…"

"Yes, sell yourself," Jake said. "Make sure they know every cool thing you can do and say everything at least twice so it sinks in. They interview a lot of people and most of them say the same old stuff. You want to be the one they remember. Listen, I gotta run but you just sit tight and wait for the phone. I've got some people in mind and they'll be calling."

"Okay, thanks," Hartman responded, his tone a mixture of gratitude and excitement.

"By the way," Jake asked. "How far away does the guy with the cane live?"

"His tent's all the way at the other end of the overpass. Why?"

"You've got some nice stuff now. Don't be flashing it around," Jake warned. "Even if it's not Gump and his cane, there's guys here who will stick you to get it."

"It's Gimp, not Gump, but good idea," Hartman admitted. "I'll keep this crap in my tent."

"You do that."

Chapter Nine
End Run

"Is this Bonnie Shelton?" the caller asked.

"Yes, who's calling?" Reeves picked up a bit of suspicion in Bonnie's voice, but maybe she was just tired of telemarketers.

"My name's Alan Reeves," he replied. "You might have heard of me. I bought the insurance brokerage you used to work for."

"I know who you are. I can't help you," was the reply. If her tone was suspicious before, it had now become frightened.

"You don't even know why I'm calling," Reeves responded. "Why would you assume I need help, and why can't you help?"

"Then you *are* asking for help. I'm not available."

"Yes, I am calling for some help," Reeves conceded. "I'm prepared to pay well. I just need some help figuring out the record-keeping system in your old brokerage."

"I spent years trying to fix the recording keeping system in 'my old brokerage' and every time I did, that man un-fixed it." First suspicious, then frightened, now the woman was sounded irritated. Even if she wouldn't come back to work for him, Reeves wanted to keep the conversation going. Maybe she'd spill some information.

"If you think anyone's mad at you, I can assure you they're not," Reeves tried. "If I thought you were responsible for the mess, I wouldn't be trying to hire you to fix it. Did I mention I'm willing to pay well?"

"Look, I'm retired," was Bonnie's reply. Suspicious to frightened to irritated and now to exasperated. "I put 25 years into a small, hometown brokerage, and I thought I knew every customer. Turns out that perhaps I didn't. I'm not sure I can help you because I'm not sure I know everything that was going on."

That statement alone confirmed Reeves' worst fears. The brokerage was making money, but he only knew that because each month the bank balance got larger. What he couldn't figure out was *how* the brokerage was making money. The books, files and records were in such bad shape he didn't know how many customers he had, what kind of insurance they'd bought, how much they were paying, and if any claims had been made. He simply deposited the checks his customers wrote, passed along the share he owed to their insurance companies, and had money left over at the end.

Reeves had been afraid to check with the insurance companies themselves. If they suspected something was amiss, they might stop letting him sell their policies. He could end up having paid good money for a business that had no products to sell.

"Just hear me out," Reeves said in a last ditch effort. "I'm not looking for hourly help. I've got that. You'd be a consultant and consultants get paid well. Your job wouldn't be to do the work, just guide the work. Help me get this all unstuck. How about just one morning- four hours? It's worth a grand to me..."

Bonnie had saved carefully and retired comfortably. But a grand was a grand. "Could you pick me up? I don't want my car parked in the lot."

"That's a bit cloak and..." Reeves started to respond, and caught himself. "Of course I can pick you up. Shall we say day after tomorrow? 8 a.m.?"

"Let's make it 6 a.m. It's still dark then," was the response. Bonnie had now run the gamut from suspicious to frightened to irritated to conspiratorial. "I don't want anybody seeing me go in with you."

Reeves forced himself to go along with her demands. The money was no big deal, apparently for either of them. If the real price of Bonnie's help was getting up earlier than usual, it would be worth it.

* * *

Reeves had promised Bonnie that she'd simply guide the work, but that wasn't her way. After taking off her coat and low-brimmed hat, she dived right in.

"Let's start with the trust account," was her directive.

In the insurance world, trust accounts are holy. When clients pay their premiums, the money goes in a broker's trust account. When it's time for the brokerage to pass that money along to the insurance company, it comes out of the trust account. Regulators were quick to investigate any anomalies in that process. For all that was wrong with the record keeping, the best chance to unstick things was as old as Watergate: follow the money.

"How about we start with some coffee?" Reeves said. "You didn't even want to go to Starbucks, but I need coffee."

"I told you," Bonnie replied. "I didn't want anybody knowing I'm here with you. I'll make some."

"No. You don't work here anymore. I have somebody to do that, and you're not her."

"The overbearing young thing out front? I like mine with cream and sugar, if you please." Bonnie had now added sarcasm to the range of voices she could project. She knew full well she'd been replaced by a millennial who probably couldn't spell insurance.

"Melissa is nice, but doesn't like being a secretary. She considers herself a broker in training," Reeves confided. Maybe he could build a bridge to Bonnie by having a common enemy. "People her age don't like paying dues the way you and I did. If she ever figures that out and gets over being offended about making coffee, I might give her a chance."

Bonnie and Reeves got to work on the trust account. It was old-school. Paper statements and cancelled checks. Each check had a policy number written in the memo section. That would be their ticket to reconciling the file folders that were in multiple drawers, sitting on credenzas and scattered on the floor.

"Did you even try to clean up this mess?" Bonnie asked.

"Remember, this was an acquisition. I already have a brokerage. Before I start folding all this into my existing operation, I've got to understand it. So I left everything exactly as it was and tried to figure it out where it sat."

The operation was helter-skelter. They'd find a cancelled check from the brokerage account, and then go through the variously scattered file folders until they found a matching policy number.

Once reconciled, the file would be piled on a desk, and they'd repeat the process with the next check.

"I don't know where this file could possibly be," Bonnie said, holding a check in her hand. "Is there by chance another pile of files in another room?"

Reeves told her he'd looked thoroughly, and all the files the brokerage owned were in the main file area. They decided to set the check aside, and move on to another one. They found that file, and soon got pretty good at matching up checks and files. But about half an hour later they found another check with no accompanying file. By the end of the four hours they were nowhere near going through the entire checkbook, but they had four checks with no accompanying files.

"Can you stay?" Reeves asked. "I'll make it $250 an hour if you'll work the rest of the day."

The hook had been sunk. Bonnie was now interested in finding answers. Her fear of being involved was being overcome by her interest in solving the puzzle.

"Yeah, I'll stay," Bonnie said. "Will Melissa run lunch for us?"

"You really like sticking it to that girl, don't you?"

"Nooo, I just don't want to go out for lunch myself. I told you I don't want anyone seeing me here. Is Maloney's still down the street? I love their subs."

Another thousand dollars and a sandwich would be a cheap price to pay for another four hours of Bonnie's knowledge. He'd buy lunch all around.

"Hey Melissa! Need you to run down to Maloney's and get us some sandwiches…Bonnie…what, an Italian?"

"Yup, Italian for me, just a half. And some chips," Bonnie said.

"Am I running lunch because I'm a young woman?" Melissa sniffed.

"No, you're running lunch because you're junior in the firm. Every business needs support people and for now that's your role."

"Allllright, two Italians and chips," she huffed. Reeves didn't see her eyes roll, but was pretty sure they had. "Will there be anything else?"

Reeves made a peace offering. "Yeah, lunch for you also."

"I'm gluten-free," was Melissa's reply. "Are their salads any good?"

"Their salads are great," Bonnie interjected. "I think they have pine nuts or feta cheese or whatever you kids have on your salads these days."

Reeves handed off two twenties and Melissa left quietly. He knew Maloney's would be busy, and he'd have time for a private chat with Bonnie. As soon as the door closed he sidled up to Bonnie.

"I gotta ask," he started plaintively. "Why are you so afraid of being seen here?"

"I still don't understand everything that went on while I worked here," she replied, speaking in a near-whisper even though they were alone. "I didn't know from day to day if I would be unemployed or in prison."

"In prison? Why on earth would you say that?" Reeves replied.

"There's lotsa different kinds of insurance fraud out there," Bonnie started to explain. "You can report something stolen that wasn't, and file a claim. You can burn something down. You can even fake car wrecks and get kickbacks from chiropractors…"

"Go on…"

"This was a life insurance brokerage," Bonnie said, leaning in closely so she could speak even more quietly. "There's only one way to commit insurance fraud if you're in the life insurance business."

"Oh that's ridiculous," Reeves exclaimed. "Worst case he could *maayybe* create false identities, and then report them dead."

"No, he couldn't," was Bonnie's reply. "Even in an age where ID theft is rampant, there's too much paperwork on a death claim. The companies look for medical records, funeral expenses and a death certificate from the state. There's no way to fake all that."

"So you actually think he was killing his clients?" Reeves was incredulous. "How did he end up with the money?"

"The only thing that fits," Bonnie whispered, "is that the 'clients' didn't know they were insured."

"Yeah, but insurance companies require an insurable interest," Reeves pointed out, a little arrogantly. After all, he was the licensed agent, she was not. "You can take out a policy on a spouse, a kid, a business partner or even an irreplaceable employee. But companies won't issue a policy on some complete stranger," he lectured.

"Insurable interest is something you *can* fake," Bonnie argued back. "Nobody checks up on it. It's stated in the application but nobody actually confirms it. You can also create a phony beneficiary. Beneficiaries aren't expected to have funeral costs, medical bills or a death certificate. Nobody expects a paper trail for the beneficiary. All the attention is on the insured."

Reeves sat back, trying to digest everything.

Bonnie continued. "I'll bet you a far more expensive lunch than Maloney's that every one of those policies we can't find has a death claim involved," she said.

"Wait a minute," Reeves shot back. "The national database. The insurance companies all report their claims. The system is built to detect fraud. If one agent had this many dead clients, somebody would notice."

"Wrong again," Bonnie patiently explained. "Only claims of $50K or more go into the database, and not all of the smaller insurance companies participate. If you kept the policies under fifty grand and shopped carefully, you might stay under the radar."

Reeves decided to do what he'd been avoiding. He'd have no choice but to log into the insurance companies' systems and check the policy numbers on the checks. He grabbed the first one from the top of the stack and fired up his computer.

"There you go. The guy's dead," Bonnie spoke while looking over Reeve's shoulder. The door opened, and they stopped talking.

"Lunch is served," Melissa said dryly. "Sorry that took so long. They screwed up the order—gave me two salads and a sandwich instead of the other way around. Boy, I gave that clerk an earful. She's got this dead end job schlepping sandwiches and she can't even get that right."

"And you're a high-powered broker-in-training who's running lunch." Reeves tried to be fatherly but was already upset. "You have no idea what's going on in that clerk's life. The true mark of a successful person is how they treat people who are less successful."

"Well, you wanted lunch and I got you lunch," Melissa said, looking at her salad. "I hope they didn't put croutons on this thing."

"Tell you what, Mel," Reeves continued. "You're not in any trouble or anything, but I'm feeling generous. How would you feel about an afternoon off?"

True to her millennial roots, Melissa jumped at the chance. For her generation, work was simply a means to an end. It paid the bills, but there was no loyalty to a business. Her work could be done tomorrow.

"That's great. I'll finish my salad at home," her coat still on from the lunch run. "I'll see you tomorrow. You did say 'with pay,' right?"

"Yes, with pay," Reeves assured her. "You have a great afternoon."

Chapter Ten
Old Boots

The phone gave its regular ring, not the "Rescue Me" ringtone of a SAR callout. But somehow Bryce knew the unidentified caller would be a deputy.

"Bryce Finn," he answered. It wasn't just any deputy.

"Hey Bryce, Bob Wright. You doin' anything this afternoon?"

"Hi, Bob. No, your timing's good," Bryce said. "We just finished finals for the quarter, and I'm headed home to de-stress."

"You and Sierra wanna de-stress in a homeless camp?" Wright asked. "Hicks and I need a cadaver dog to work a homicide scene."

Bryce might not have been wild about Hicks, but he especially hated, *hated,* homeless camps. He was sympathetic to the homeless themselves, but had a big problem with their personal hygiene. Camps were usually littered with garbage, needles, broken glass and rusty beer cans. Worse, some residents didn't have the manners of a cat. He'd had to decontaminate his boots and Sierra's feet more than once.

"Looking for a weapon, I suppose," Bryce asked back. "A knife or something like that? If you know it's a homicide then I guess you have the body."

"We do. Guy was stabbed to death," Wright said. "We'd like to find the weapon, maybe tossed in the brush, maybe in one of the nearby tents. These things are usually beefs between campers."

"We'll be over," Bryce said. "Which camp?" It was telling that even in a small county like Kitsap, there were multiple homeless camps that could have been in play. "Wait—303 and McWilliams?"

"So far so good," Wright said. "But if we're playing games you gotta guess which corner."

That stumped Bryce. He had searched the one behind the grocery store a couple of times, and wasn't aware of a second. "There's more than one now?" he asked. "Okay, I'll bite. It's not the one behind the grocery store...wherever it is."

"I'll give you that," Wright said. "It's right across the street, behind the park and ride. You'll see our rigs."

The trip to meet the two detectives took a bit longer than usual. When he stopped by the house to get Sierra, Bryce rummaged through the garage and found an old pair of boots. The soles were nearly coming off, but he'd kept them for just such a situation.

The first time he'd been to a homeless camp, some ground pounders literally got the dirty end of the stick. They'd been digging up what they thought was a possible grave, and realized far too late that they were excavating the camp's former latrine. There was no amount of steam cleaning or bleach that would make any of their boots wearable again. Every single member of that team submitted claims to the state for new boots, and when the bureaucrat in charge of SAR heard why, he cut the checks in record time.

Bryce parked along the east side of the lot, adjacent to a patch of thick woods that he presumed held a homeless camp, and a murder scene.

"Welcome to the street of dreams," was Hicks' greeting. Wright's SUV was there, but he was not in sight. "You'll love what they've done with the place."

"I doubt it," Bryce answered back. "I'm not much into interior decorating, especially not with needles and beer cans."

"This would be 'exterior' decorating, but you're right about the décor," Hicks said, each of them trying to one-up the other's sarcasm. "They accessorize with empty potato chip bags."

"And the occasional human 'land mine.'" Bryce shot back.

"I've been out there, and it's not too bad in that respect," Hicks said. "I didn't smell anything and didn't see any piles."

Bryce desperately needed to change the subject. "I assume Bob...Sgt. Wright...is down at the scene? He said we were looking for a knife?"

"Well, probably a knife," Hicks replied. "If it's a knife it's a big one, or maybe even a machete. No autopsy yet, but it was pretty obvious the wounds were deep. We want to see if the killer tossed whatever he used while fleeing the area."

"How much blood at the scene itself?" was Bryce's next question.

"A ton," Hicks said. "The guy got cut all to hell, and there's blood everywhere."

"Can we take a look without Sierra?" Bryce was already formulating a search strategy. He knew it might be difficult finding a knife stained with a little bit of blood right next to a tent with a lot of blood. The odor from one might overwhelm the other. He knew it could be done—in fact, he'd actually done it— but it required a very careful approach.

The two joined Wright at the scene, and there was indeed blood everywhere. The good news was that the crime lab types were packing up the tent and the dead man's belongings. Most of the blood was on the tent and his sleeping bag, not the ground. That meant one big source of odor would be leaving.

The lab techs would have a much more difficult job than Sierra. Sierra's job was to find blood and by extension the murder weapon, somewhere at the scene. She didn't care whose blood, so long as it was human.

The lab techs, on the other hand, needed to check every single spatter of blood on every single thing in and around the tent. People who kill with edged weapons almost invariably cut themselves. The lab's job would be to find that little sploch of blood that didn't belong to the victim and would hopefully identify the killer.

"Let's do this," Bryce said. "While these guys are clearing out, let's get Sierra and work the trails and other campsites. That way we'll find anything that's been tossed on the way out. Once the air has cleared a bit, we'll come back here and detail this area."

"Whatever." Hicks wasn't excited by the death of yet another homeless dude. It was his opinion that all of them were killing themselves anyway, with booze, drugs and unprotected sex. The only thing a murder did was accelerate the process.

Bryce got Sierra out of the car, and began to search an area completely outside the detectives' area of interest. He told her to "find Digger," and then went in the opposite direction of where everyone was working.

"Hey kid, what're you doin'? You know we're working over here, right?" Hicks asked. Bryce had put Sierra in a strip of grass just off the parking lot, well away from the homeless camp.

"Yup. But she was in her run pen all day, and now in the truck. I want to let her burn a little energy off before we search the area we care about," Bryce explained. "Let's let her get her ya-yas out here, where there's nothing."

Sierra worked the strip at top speed, down to the fence at the other end, and had started back when she suddenly dynamited her little doggie brakes. Her head snapped back and she returned to an area she'd already passed twice.

"You sure this area's not involved?" Bryce whispered. He didn't want to distract Sierra by talking too loudly.

Hicks didn't get the hint, and spoke in a normal voice. "It's nothin'. The scene's down below."

Sierra put her nose to the ground and then sat. Bryce walked up to see what had gotten Sierra's interest, and noticed a glove. The mate was nearby.

"It's nothin'," Hicks responded. "People lose gloves all the time getting in and out of their cars."

Bryce knew Hicks didn't like input, but couldn't help pushing back. "I know, but this is different. They lose their gloves in parking spaces, not over the guard rail. These have been tossed. Plus, both gloves are here. I've found lots of gloves on searches and never found a pair. People lose one glove or the other, but they don't lose entire pairs. That makes me think they were ditched. Sierra's alerted on them, you ought to collect them. I mean, you've got the lab here anyway."

"Waste of time," Hicks said firmly. He wasn't about to take advice from somebody who was both a teenager and a volunteer. "The lab's got enough to do without picking up gloves willy nilly off the edge of a parking lot. And Wright and I are on overtime so let's get moving."

Bryce gave Sierra a mild reward. He was pretty sure there was blood on at least the one glove. He also quietly touched a button on his GPS that would mark the location. But in the end he did as told, and the two men walked down to where the murder had occurred.

"Hey, Bryce, glad you could join us." Despite standing next to a death scene, Wright was perfectly jolly. "Thanks for coming out."

"Good to be here," was Bryce's automatic reply, rooted in politeness. He stopped immediately and corrected himself. "Well, not good that somebody's dead, but always good to see you guys...you know what I mean."

"Yeah, no worries. I knew whatcha meant." Wright shrugged off the comment, knowing that for people who work death scenes, normal pleasantries are just simply...normal.

Wright continued. "I saw you two earlier checking out the rest of the place."

"Yeah, we'll let Sierra work the other side while the lab techs wrap up here," Bryce explained. "I assume you've searched the immediate area for weapons? It'd be really hard for Sierra to pick out a knife or something with this much blood right nearby."

"Uh-huh. We did a 25 foot circle around the tent just to see if something was dumped right there, Wright said. "We're really looking for Sierra to check the other paths and escape routes."

"Well, that we can do," Bryce said, turning his attention to Sierra. "Wanna go find some Digger, girl? Yes, let's find Digger."

Bryce walked through the brush behind Sierra, his hands in his pockets. Even though that affected his balance and made it more likely he'd trip and fall, he worked hard to keep his body language completely neutral.

To that end, Bryce always faced Sierra and kept his belly button pointed at her. That way if she did turn around at look at him, she'd always see the same thing. Shoulders slumped, hands in pockets, no expression on his face. Bryce also kept moving, so as not to signal that he had interest in some particular spot. If Sierra stopped to explore an area, Bryce might even move sideways. His goal was to never stop moving while Sierra was searching.

It didn't take long for Sierra to find an area to explore. They were on the complete opposite side of the homeless camp, and Sierra was working toward a tent in the distance. She was snorting, sniffing first the air and then the ground, and moving back and forth.

"See her 'working the cone,'" Bryce said softly to Wright, who had chosen to follow them. "She's got something over there, probably by that tent. I'd kind of expected her to find something more remote...in the bushes, if the bad guy tossed his weapon."

"Let it play out," Wright replied. "I know the guy who lives there, and he's worth a look."

The cone that Sierra worked got smaller and smaller, and was pointed right at the tent. She broke out of the brush and into a small clearing around the tent. Her head snapped and she snorted to clear her sinuses, and then she moved directly toward the tent.

"Who the hell is out there?" came a voice from inside, angry. Sierra was startled, and moved back from the tent, looking at Bryce.

"Gimp, it's Bob Wright. We've got a dog with us, but she's friendly."

Gimp unzipped the tent flap and stuck his head out. "I don't give a crap who it is, or if the dog's friendly. Get the hell out of my camp."

"Gimp, it's me. Bob Wright...from the Sheriff's Office. I helped ya out when those guys tried to jump you, remember."

"I remember you, and that doesn't give you the right to march in here slobbering the place up with a dog," Gimp retorted. "I don't know who you're looking for, but I'm the only one here."

"It's not a who, it's a what," Wright replied, trying to soften his tone. "You heard about Eddie, right?"

"Yeah...what's that got to do with me?"

"Well, did you hear anything?" Wright figured if he could get Gimp talking, he'd forget there was a dog sniffing around. He also wanted to see Gimp's hands. "Come on out here and talk to me."

Gimp did as he was told. He'd had enough contacts with the police to know they didn't usually change their minds. He'd been physically dragged from his tent before.

"Step over here, if you would," Wright asked, changing to a softer tone. Gimp attempted to move in Wright's direction but could hardly walk without his cane. When he got closer, Wright popped the big question. "What do you remember from last night?"

"That I was completely lip-walking drunk, right there in my tent," Gimp said. It was certainly believable. Wright knew that booze, not drugs, was Gimp's thing. But while he stuck to a legal drug, he consumed it in quantities that would kill most people outright.

"Did you finish that all last night?" Wright asked, pointing to a gallon of vodka just inside the tent.

"Most of it. I saved a little for hair-of-the-dog." Gimp started to laugh. "And damned if we don't have a real dog in here. Good lookin' mutt." Gimp's attitude was changing. "What's she sniffin' for?"

"Blood," Wright explained. Sierra was now clearly interested in the tent. She snorted, made a lap around the tent and then returned to the unzipped door. She never set foot inside, but sat and stared intently at the open flap.

"You cut yourself or anything, buddy?" Hicks asked, surprising everyone with his presence. He'd been remarkably quiet working his way through the brush to join them.

"Who're you?" Gimp asked. Before Hicks could reply Wright jumped in. "He's a detective who works for me." He turned to let

Hicks see the annoyed look on his face. "Waylon, let's not pepper the man with questions. I've got this."

"I thought it was my case, but whatever," was Hicks' comeback. That would earn him another conversation later.

The question itself was a good one, but tricky. Gimp wasn't in custody, and the detectives could ask general questions without running afoul of Gimp's Miranda rights. But the moment they focused on him as a suspect they'd have to Mirandize him, and the conversation would likely be over.

Wright turned back to Gimp. "So is there any explanation for why the dog thinks there's blood in your tent?" Wright asked in the most non-accusatory tone he could muster.

"No…didn't crap or puke neither," Gimp added defensively. "That was good vodka, didn't make me sick like the cheaper stuff."

"Can we look?" Wright asked, seeking consent to search. He could screw up Miranda, but if he got consent to search and found a weapon that part would hold up.

"You're gonna do what you're gonna do," Gimp said.

"Is that a 'Yes?'" Wright persisted.

"I *said* yes, I haven't done anything. Do whatever you need to so you can move on."

Wright nodded at Bryce, who held open the tent flap for Sierra. She started to go in, but stopped and stepped back. She put her nose down just inside the tent. Gimp's cane was laying there, between the lip of the tent door and his sleeping bag.

"Good girl," Bryce told Sierra. "It's okay, go on in."

Sierra hopped inside and snorted around a bit. There were obviously plenty of smells inside it wouldn't take a dog to find. But after making a lap of the tent Sierra came back to the door, again nosed the cane, and sat.

"Why would my dog be interested in your cane?" Bryce asked. On one hand, he was out of line for questioning a suspect. On the other hand, in an effort to explain his dog's behavior, maybe he could ask questions that would be out of bounds for police.

"Hell if I know," Gimp said. "Who knows what kinda crap I've stuck the end of that thing in?"

Bryce gave Sierra a mild "good girl," brought her out of the tent and looked at Wright.

"Can I talk to you over here for a minute?" He asked.

"Sure," Wright replied. The two stepped a few trees away while Hicks continued making small talk with Gimp.

"Sierra's not alerting on the bottom of the cane," Bryce told Wright. "She put her nose on the handle end. There's a seam or something right below the handle. It's almost like there's something collected in the seam."

"Okay, thanks" Wright responded. He walked over to the tent, but turned toward Gimp. "You did give us permission to search the tent, right?"

"Yeah, I guess so. But maybe…"

"Thankyew!" was Wright's immediate reply as he snatched the cane from the tent. "You smack anybody with this?"

"No way. Hey…what're you trying to say?" Gimp appeared defensive, but didn't end the search.

Wright held the cane by the shaft, the curved handle up in the air. "I think this would be a great weapon for beating somebody," he said. He had no thoughts that Gimp was actually the murderer. But putting him on the hot seat might make him cough up information. As part of his intimidation act, he raised the cane over his head and brought it down on an imaginary victim.

To the surprise of everyone but Gimp, the handle moved. The seam Bryce mentioned had opened to a two-inch gap. Wright grabbed the handle and pulled the two sections apart, revealing the hidden blade.

To the surprise of everyone including Gimp, there was a large amount of blood toward the tip, and a smaller smear near the handle. Wright dropped the cane and drew his own weapon.

"Gimp, I need you to turn around and face away from me, hands in the air," Wright said calmly. There was no need to scream like the cops on TV. In a normal voice he simply added, "If you reach for anything, I'll shoot you."

Gimp tried to get down on his knees but his leg injury prevented it. He fell flat on his face into some blackberries, yelping in pain but keeping his hands visible. Wright and Hicks pulled him out of the stickers, to the accompaniment of more yelps, and got him handcuffed.

"Alright, buddy. Let's go," Hicks interjected. He began dragging the limping man through the brush, back to his car. "Boss, I think we've got our killer."

"Wait…what?" Gimp said. "I already told you guys I was passed out in my tent last night. I didn't beat nobody and I sure as hell didn't stab nobody."

Hicks stared directly at Wright. "All that blood will be a cinch to match to our victim." He was walking a knife-edge sharper than the murder weapon. Hicks was not asking questions. He was talking to Wright, but trying to provoke Gimp into what the courts call an "excited utterance." It was borderline dirty pool.

Everyone who's ever watched more than one or two cop shows on TV can recite the Miranda warning by heart. But behind all the explicit, court-ordered language, the Miranda warning contains an implicit message: "I'm trying to send you to prison. You're an idiot if you talk to me."

"Hicks, just get him up in the car and get him Mirandized." Wright was more than happy to play dirty pool if it would get a killer off the streets. He just didn't have confidence that Hicks could pull off the trick.

"Hey…guys. I'll talk to ya," Gimp said. "I got nothin' to hide. I liked Eddie. Him and me had no beefs. Why would I kill him?"

"Let's get you up in the car and get the formalities done, and then you can tell us your story," Hicks said.

Wright gloved up and began to collect the cane. He pondered whether to put the blade back in the straight part of the cane, or try to secure them separately. As he stood looking, Bryce stepped closer.

"Can I talk to you for a second?" he asked Wright.

"Sure." Wright never had any trouble taking input from Bryce.

"When I was warming up Sierra in the parking lot, she hit on a glove. Both the left and right were there, and they'd been tossed over the guard rail. I think you oughta collect them."

"Did ya tell Hicks?" Wright asked.

"Yes. He ignored me," Bryce said. "He wouldn't pick 'em up. Look, I'm already on Hicks' bad side, and I don't want any more grief from him. But I felt like I had to tell you."

"Damn right, you did." Wright's tone had changed, and Bryce detected that he was a bit hot. "Look, I'm going to share something with you that you can't tell anyone. And like it or not, you always have to treat Hicks with respect. You're a volunteer."

"Okaaay." Bryce wasn't sure what was coming.

"Hicks is the suckiest detective I've ever had working for me. I'm sorry I wasn't up in the lot to greet you. It never dawned on me that he could even foul that up."

"I don't want to get him in trouble or cause you any grief," Bryce said meekly.

"People make their own trouble," Wright said. "You're not the problem and if *you* get any grief down the road I want you to tell me. We'll get the gloves when we get back to the lot, and I'll talk to Hicks back at the office so you're not around."

"Thank you," Bryce said, looking back at the blade. "Interesting pattern."

"What?" Wright asked.

"Lots of blood down by the business end, then a clean spot, then more blood up by the handle," Bryce pointed out. "Funny how blood spurts and sprays, hits here, misses there."

"Good point," Wright said, apparently deep in thought. He'd decided to put the blade back in the cane, to make it safer to handle on the way to the lab. Bryce watched him do that.

"Wait a minute," Bryce said. "Sliding in like that, shouldn't the blood have smeared all the way to the top?"

"Yeah, I guess so," Wright said, wondering.

Bryce pressed on. "Wouldn't that mean the blood was mostly dry before it went back in the sheath? I mean…if it didn't smear?"

Wright decided to let his youngest detective play things out. "Okay, go on."

"Look, Hicks had to help Gimp even on the trail. He clearly can't walk without a cane. If he'd gone up there and stabbed your victim, he'd have needed the cane to get back here. He'd have put the blade back in right away."

"Soooo?" Wright wasn't following.

"I get fresh drawn blood all the time for cadaver training," Bryce explained. "When you go to the doctor they put something in it to keep in from clotting, it stays liquid. But without that it clots almost immediately. I have a heck of a time smearing it on something to test Sierra. It's completely dry in just a few minutes."

"What're you thinking?" Wright continued to press.

"Not sure I've completely figured it out. I just know that Gimp needed the assembled cane to get back to his camp, and if he'd have shoved the blade back in right away he'd have smeared blood down the whole length."

Wright was catching on. "I'm not an expert on blood spatter. Does it dry quickly enough that someone could have walked it back to Gimp's tent before sheathing it?"

"Pretty close in my experience," Bryce offered. "Wouldn't the lab guys be able to tell you?"

"Yeah, I'll get them on that. You really think somebody besides Gimp could have done this?"

Bryce was beginning to believe his own theory. "If Gimp had tried walking back to camp just leaning on the blade, it would have sunk into the ground. But if he'd sheathed the cane right after stabbing somebody, he'd have smeared blood the whole length. However it happened, somebody waited a while before putting that blade back into the cane.

"Jeez, you're right," Wright said. He headed out the trail toward the parking lot. "Hicks better hope nobody's screwed with those gloves."

Chapter Eleven
Two R'd Darryl

"Two guys named Darryl decide to go for a hike?' Sounds like the start of a really bad joke." Deputy Lee Fuller would be in charge of the day's search, and his forehead was already furrowed. "Darryl and his brother Darryl walk into a bar…"

"Well, actually they did." Ed Lindsey was Jones' counterpart from the Forest Service and had taken the initial missing person report. "They weren't brothers though. One spells his name Daryl with one "R" and the missing guy is Darryl-with-two-R's."

"You're kidding," Jones replied. "So the two of them stagger out of a bar and into the woods and only one of them comes back?"

"Right. The one who didn't have a head injury," Fuller said, further complicating the story. "Our missing Darryl-with-two-R's fell off his bar stool earlier in the binge. He landed on his head, but medics apparently cleared him so they staggered out together."

"And into the woods. My woods. On a weekend when I have SAR duty." Fuller liked solving mysteries, but he could already sense this one would be a disappointment. "What I'd give for a couple of hikers who just took a wrong turn and got lost."

"Sorry," Lindsey replied. "We work with what we have."

"I'll get SAR started this way, but first lets you and I take a walk out the main trail at least. Maybe he's down alongside," Fuller said, reaching for his radio. "178, Westcom. Can you start a SAR callout for me? I don't have good cell service here."

"*Received, 178,*" the dispatcher responded. "*We'll get 'em going and let you know what's coming. You want ground pounders and dogs I presume?*"

"178, add the ATV team to that. We'll need to transport teams around and the roads are pretty bumpy."

"*Got it. Ground pounders, K9 and the four-by guys. Check back in twenty.*"

Fuller and Lindsey started down the River Trail, one checking each side in the brush. There was no visible sign of Darryl. At the 20 minute mark dispatch came back to report 15 ground pounders, three dog teams and two members of the county 4X4 unit were en route.

"Thanks, radio," was Fuller's reply. "Text them to just wait at the trailhead parking lot if I'm not back when they get here."

"*Aaaat the trailhead parking lot. Reeeceived,*" was the dispatcher's reply. Drawing out vowels was her way of being a hipster dispatcher. All the cool ones did that.

* * *

"We're looking for Darryl," was Fuller's briefing to the assembled SAR members. "Darryl decided he didn't want to continue hiking with his buddy Daryl and was supposedly headed back for the parking lot. He hasn't been seen since."

Katie was the first to jump in. "Why was he hiking if he had a head injury?"

"Alcohol," Fuller replied. "He'd quite literally fallen off a bar stool earlier, been cleared by medics, and the two of them had the bright idea of going hiking."

"And we're sure he just wandered off?" came the question from Bryce.

"If you're asking whether somebody did him in, we've considered it. In the meantime, we're going to take the other Daryl at his word and start a search."

Bryce and Sierra would be assigned the high-probability area where two-R was last seen. The odds were that if the man had a truly serious brain injury, he wouldn't have gotten too far. He'd have gotten sleepy, laid down in nearby brush, and died.

Katie and Magnum would continue out the trail, and search both sides further out. The dividing line between their assignments was a creek system which dumped into the Union River. In some places it was a single large stream, and in others it was three smaller channels. They'd each search from the river to a ridgeline about a quarter mile away.

Bryce unclipped Sierra's leash and stashed it in a slash pocket on his rain pants. Before he could even begin to say "go find," Sierra was off. The trail curved uphill to the left, but Bryce stepped into the brush and followed the shoreline of the river. He'd have Sierra work the banks and brush to start, and then work up toward the ridgeline. He expected it to take a couple of hours to cover their assigned area, and Katie just a little longer to cover hers.

As usual, just about the time they began searching it started to rain. Bryce heard some thunder in the distance, but unless the storm got a lot closer he wouldn't worry. In western Washington, searching in the rain was a given.

Sierra had zero interest along the riverbank and along the first pass inland. A second inland pass, closer to the trail, produced some interest. Bryce surmised Sierra was reacting to the many human scents that were drifting down from the trail. She never zeroed in on a spot, or even started working a scent pool. She kept moving further and further away, but with no real focus.

"44, 66," came Katie's call over the radio.

Bryce keyed his mic and responded. "44..."

"What's the rain activity been since our subject went missing? This creek bed's dry now, but what if it was raining when he went down? Could his body have been swept downstream?"

"Good thought," Bryce replied. "What's Magnum doing?"

"He kinda wants to work this creek system, that's why I asked. It's slick and rocky, but I think I'll follow him."

"Following your dog is always a good idea," Bryce said, trying to avoid sarcasm on the radio.

"66, clear." And Katie began making her way down the creek bed. It wound around, broke into multiple channels, rejoined and then split again, all in its journey to the Union River. Katie and Magnum would have to check all of sections, to see if the missing man had gotten hung up in bushes. In places the banks were pretty high, meaning high water could have left two-R'd Darryl entangled well above their heads.

The thunder continued in the distance but seemed far enough away, and Bryce wasn't worried about lightning. Katie's change of plan required him to adjust his own. He would now work Sierra up to the top of the ridgeline, as far from Katie and Magnum as possible. By the time they got back down toward the river, Katie would have finished her own sweep to the creek's mouth.

"Wow, it's really starting to come down," Bryce thought to himself. "This hill's going to get muddy."

Sierra never missed a beat. Golden Retrievers love mud almost as much as they love water. Some of Bryce's teammates had teased him by calling Sierra a "swamp collie," and Bryce knew they weren't far off. He spent about 20 minutes getting to the top of the ridgeline, and would work back and forth on the way down. That would put him far from Katie and Magnum while still covering his assignment.

Bryce worked the far corner of his area, letting Sierra range out and do most of the work. She was having a great time in the rain and mud, but showing no signs of smelling anything.

"44, 66" came Katie's voice over the radio. Bryce knew her well enough to pick up a note of concern.

"44, go ahead."

"44, 66…all this rain is causing the creek to rise. I'm out in the middle of a wide spot and not sure I can get back to the bank."

"Why can't you get to the bank?" Bryce asked, not realizing Katie was at the confluence of three channels that drained into the river. Katie had quickly tired of walking on slick rocks, and when a sandy spot appeared in the middle of the confluence, she shifted to walking on it. But now, just a few inches of water were turning her place of refuge into quicksand. She was a good 50 to 75 feet away from anything approaching dry land.

"My boots are getting stuck in the sand," was Katie's next radio call, with a bit more urgency. *"If this gets much higher, they'll overtop and fill."*

Bryce abandoned his search assignment and began moving in Katie's direction. The rain and mud slowed his own progress, and he wasn't exactly sure where the three channels came together. Small creeks typically shift paths from year to year, and Bryce knew his map was probably not accurate.

Worse, Bryce could now hear the sound of rushing water. He realized the problem wasn't the rain that was falling on them, but the huge thunderstorm he'd heard miles away. That water had flowed off a faraway mountain and he had no clue how deep the approaching rush might be. Six inches or three feet, it would arrive in whatever depth Mother Nature chose. And Katie was mired in a place where not one, but three channels would be collecting water.

"Kaayy-tee!!" Bryce yelled, trying to get a fix on his teammate's location. The brush along the banks was incredibly thick and Bryce was afraid he wouldn't be able to see her.

"66, 44, I just gave you a voice check. Hear anything?"

"66, nothing. Water's at mid-calf. At least Magnum made it to the bank."

"Magnum, come!" was Bryce's next step. It would be turning a search problem around backwards, but maybe Magnum could lead him to Katie. Bryce tried again. "Magnum! Come."

After a short time the bushes in front of Bryce began to shift, meaning either a bear or Magnum was coming at them. It turned out to indeed be Magnum, and Bryce took the leap.

"Magnum," he said. "Where's Katie? Show me."

Nothing. Magnum was used to the "show me" command coming from Katie. He only stared at Bryce.

"Magnum! Where's Katie? Can you take me to Katie?"

Magnum turned and ran back into the bushes he'd just left. He stopped, turned around at looked at Bryce, with his head cocked. It was the universal canine body language for a question mark.

"Good boy," Bryce said, softly this time. He took a single step in Magnum's direction to signal that it was okay to go.

Magnum was gone. Now Bryce's problem was keeping up in the thick brush, but he knew it wouldn't be far and that he'd likely pop out within sight of Katie. The good news was that Sierra had taken off after Magnum, so both were crushing brush, clearing a path.

As he expected, it didn't take long to break out of the brush, and almost fall in the water himself. Over the years the stream had undercut the bank, so the thick brush hung over the water. Both dogs were swimming toward Katie, and Bryce could see water now almost to her knees.

"Can you get loose?" Bryce yelled over the sound of the rushing water.

"One foot's loose because it just came out of my boot," Katie yelled back. She was still on the sandbar-turned-quicksand, and now with one stocking foot.

"Drop your pack," Bryce hollered.

"I can't get it back," Katie replied, misunderstanding. "It's down in the mud. I'll just have to go barefoot on one side."

"Nooo," Bryce hollered even louder, pointing over his own shoulder. "Drop your pack...your PACK! It's weighing you down."

Sometimes when people are in dire straits, stubbornness kicks in. Katie was one of those. "I've already lost a boot," she yelled back. "I don't wanna lose my pack." Even as the water rose, she refused to drop the 35 pounds of dead weight strapped to her back.

About that time, Bryce noticed that both Magnum and Sierra were levitating in the moving water, about 20 feet from Katie. So far as he knew, neither dog was Jesus.

"Look at the dogs. There's gotta be a boulder or something they're standing on. The water's only a couple inches deep there. Can you get that far?" Bryce tried coaxing.

"My foot's really stuck. Have you got a rope or something?"

"All I've got is paracord," Bryce offered. The newer paracord was rated to lift or pull 550 pounds, but was far too lightweight to throw like a traditional rope. The wind would simply blow it away. Even if the paracord would work to pull Katie out, the hard part would be getting her an end to grab.

Bryce looked around and found a long, thick branch. He quickly broke two pieces over his knee—and tied one piece to each end of the cord. If this worked, each of them would be like skiers at the end of a tow rope. Bryce would simply need to walk backwards, and hope the ultra-light paracord material could stand the strain.

Bryce's toss was just a little bit short, and the stick landed in the water. It began to drift downstream, well out of Katie's reach. She almost went face down in the water trying to get it.

But Bryce had forgotten one important thing—an opportunity, really. He'd tossed a stick in the water, right in front of two Golden Retrievers! Both Sierra and Magnum dived off their boulder, racing each other to the stick. Sierra was by far the better swimmer, and got the stick in her mouth first.

"Here, Sierra," Katie called. "Bring me the stick." But Sierra was Bryce's dog, and was used to retrieving for him.

"Sierra...nooo...bring ME the stick," Katie tried again. Bryce saw what was developing and decided to take a risk. He stepped back into the brush, so that Sierra could no longer see him. That way Katie would be the only person around that could throw the stick again.

The trick worked. Sierra turned and started swimming toward Katie, the stick still in her mouth and the paracord floating behind.

"Good girl," Katie said to Sierra. "Hon, Sierra's here. Grab your end and pull."

Bryce stepped into view again, and to his frustration, now couldn't find *his* end. He realized that when Sierra took one end toward Katie, the other end had tangled and slipped off the bank. The stick that was to have been Bryce's end of the tow rope was now itself headed downstream.

"Magnum, can you get the stick?" Bryce said, pointing downstream. Magnum understood "stick," and better yet saw a chance to get the stick before his sister. With dogs, it's not about the having, it's about the getting. Beating Sierra was all that mattered, and Magnum had the stick in no time. Now, the problem was reversed. Magnum was used to retrieving for Katie, and that stick needed to go to Bryce.

Squeak! Squeak! came the noise from Bryce's vest. He knew Magnum loved squeakies, so squeezing Sierra's ball would have the desired effect. So long as Magnum brought the stick, he didn't care if Sierra followed.

Turned out Bryce was two-for-two on bright ideas. Magnum swam right up to the bank where he was standing, looking for a squeaky toy. Bryce grabbed the stick, and began walking backward. The tiny line tightened, and now they'd see if it would actually live up to its much-advertised 550 pounds.

"See if you can hook your foot back in the boot, maybe we can rescue it too," Bryce yelled. "Try to avoid any yanks or jerks. Let's just pull you steadily out of there."

The two worked slowly, and the foot that was still stuck started to work loose. But Katie uttered a rare expletive.

"Dammit, the loose boot just got washed away. When it came out of the mud it slipped off my toe."

"No worries," Bryce reassured. "We'll get somebody to bring you shoes from the truck. Slow now…let's gently get you across these rocks."

"Now that I'm out of the mud, you almost don't need to pull. Thank God the rocks are rounded. There's nothing sharp on my foot." Katie made her way easily to shore, climbed the embankment and flopped down next to Bryce. Only then did she realize how much of a toll the water had taken.

"I'm freezing," she said. "And we aren't going anywhere till somebody gets here with shoes. It's one thing to walk barefoot on polished river rock, but there's nothing but stickers along that path."

"I think maybe you'll be okay," Bryce responded, not looking at Katie at all. His eyes were focused out in the still rising creek, and the Golden Retriever swimming their way.

"She's got my boot!" Katie cried. Sierra was indeed living up to the retriever name. The space age material in Katie's boot made it light enough to float, and Sierra had recovered it. It was sopping wet, but would still work to get Katie out of the woods. They'd have to explain why they didn't finish their assignment, but they'd have a terrific war story to tell.

Katie laced up the recovered boot as Sierra looked on. No toy for this "find," but Sierra was getting lots of praise and pets. "Now where's Magnum?" Katie asked. Her answer was a series of barks a few dozen yards downstream.

It was unmistakably Magnum, but the barks were different than Katie had ever heard. They had a high pitch, almost as if Magnum was frightened. Both humans feared he'd gotten his collar caught on a snag, and might even be drowning. They almost tripped over each other following the sound, and broke out of thick brush at the same time.

As it turned out, Magnum was fine. But two-R'd-Darryl wasn't. He was upside down, hung up in the creekside brush, his shirttail almost obscuring his face. Between that and decomposition, he didn't look human. Bryce and Katie assumed that's what had freaked out Magnum. He'd found their man.

Katie handled rewarding Magnum, and Sierra too. Showing up with Katie and Bryce, the older search dog made a find just like her little brother, so they both got love. Bryce got on the radio to let base know they'd found their man.

"Roger, 44. Base copies you've met up with Nat Sessions and will be taking a break. We copy those coordinates and I think one of the detectives wants to come out and chat with you both."

"Did they say 'detective?'" Katie asked.

"I think so," Bryce said, keying up his radio. "Copy on the detective, base. 44 clear."

"Base clear."

"Jeez, do you think it'll be Hicks?" Katie asked as the two sat, waiting. "I was really hoping not to run in to him again."

Bryce was philosophical. "We'll have to run into him sooner or later. We don't have the luxury of only dealing with people we like."

Nothing more was said, until the sound of footsteps broke the silence. As they peered through the bushes, their fears were realized.

"Hi guys," Hicks said.

"Hi detective," Bryce responded. Katie spoke volumes by offering no greeting of her own.

The silence drew Hicks' attention to Katie. "What'd you do, fall in the creek? You're soaked."

"We go where our dogs go," Katie shrugged, offering no details of what really transpired.

"Well, it's time for you and your dogs to *go* back to base," Hicks said, turning to Bryce. "Unless you've got a pair of gloves to show me."

"I wasn't trying to get you in trouble on that, sir," Bryce responded. "I just trust my dog."

"Just trust that if you keep getting crossways with us detectives your career in SAR will come to a quick end," Hicks said.

"It's not detectives plural, sir. It's detective singular, as in you," Bryce said. "We get along fine with everybody else. If you'd like to sit down with Bob Wright and hash this out, I'd be happy to do that. In the meantime, we'll head back to base and get this written up. And whether you want to join us or not, I will be discussing this with Bob."

"You sniveling little snot…" was all Hicks could snarl.

"Have a nice day, sir," was Bryce's final word as he, Katie and the dogs moved out. "As you requested, we'll head back to base and get this written up."

Bryce and Katie made the trip in silence. Once at base they hooked up with Deputy Fuller to do their paperwork.

"You guys okay?" the deputy asked. "You seem bummed. I can call a chaplain if this one is bothering you."

"We're fine," Bryce said, barely getting the words out of his mouth.

"We're NOT fine," Katie interjected. "That Detective Hicks is still giving Bryce crap over getting him in trouble. He's always been a grump and the last two times we've had to work with him he's been just plain mean."

Fuller raised his eyebrows. "I heard something after the last search, but there's always some kind of rumor going around. Been a real jerk, huh?"

"Yes!" Katie said, before Bryce could rejoin the conversation. "He doesn't seem to appreciate anything we do."

At just that moment, Gary Manning approached with a team of 10 ground pounders and a litter. "We're ready to do the recovery, Lee. We copied the coordinates when Bryce radioed them in."

"Thanks," Fuller replied...and then thought for a moment. He gave Katie a sideways smile before continuing. "On second thought it'll be at least an hour, maybe two, before the coroner gets here. I'd really hate to make you all stand around and wait. You can pack up and head on home."

Manning was confused. "But who's gonna..."

"Hicks is a trained and savvy detective," Fuller replied. "He'll figure something out."

No longer confused, Manning was incredulous. "You're just gonna leave..." and stopped when he saw Fuller key his radio mic.

"178, Westcom. All SAR units will be clear of this scene, including myself. Detective Hicks is on-site, awaiting arrival of the coroner."

Unkeying, he looked directly at Katie and Bryce. "Detective Hicks, it just became 'leg day' at the Wilderness Gym."

Chapter Twelve
Teddy Bear Picnic

"If you go down in the woods today you're sure of a big surprise.
If you go down in the woods today you'd better be in disguise.
For every bear there ever was will gather there for certain because
Today's the day the teddy bears have their picnic."
(© 1932 "Teddy Bear Picnic" Jimmy Kennedy, Fair Use.)

The nice thing about gathering scent articles is that it's also a chance to gather information. Handlers are escorted by family around the house, looking for clothing or other soft items a missing subject had recently used. That gives them a chance to make small talk with family members, without the cops around.

Bryce had gotten very good at this, despite his young age—or perhaps because of it. He was 18 and not in uniform. He was the epitome of "not the cops."

"So he's 33-years old, but has the mental capacity of a two-year old?" Bryce asked as he and the missing man's caregiver went through the foster home.

"That's what we were told," she said. The home was off-grid, in rural Kitsap County. "He's only been here a couple days, but seems very gentle with the toddlers. We've already started letting them play together while we work the garden."

Bryce held his tongue, knowing all the reasons why a 33-year-old mentally-challenged person shouldn't be playing alone with toddlers. However, as a searcher, Bryce's only role was to find the man, not fix the family.

"Did you have an argument or anything? Why would he leave?" He made a mental note to suggest the deputy talk to the other kids alone. Maybe the missing man had a reason to get out of Dodge.

The caregiver was adamant. "No, like I told the officer, we saw him last night before bed. He seemed happy and was enjoying the place. We assumed he was in his room all night but when he didn't come down this morning we checked and he was gone."

Bryce continued going through the room, struggling to find scent articles because the man was new to the home. All of his clothing had been recently donated. There were sacks and sacks of clothing in the room, not one stitch of which had ever been worn.

"I washed all his dirty clothes when he got here," the caregiver said. "Some of it was so bad I had to throw it out." That meant it was comingled with garbage. If Bryce tried to use something from the garbage can as a scent article, the dogs could end up searching for a ham sandwich.

"Pillowcase?" Bryce asked.

"His family didn't send over a pillow. We're getting him one soon," was the response.

Bryce tried again. "Toothbrush?"

"Hasn't brushed since he's been here."

Bryce was about to grab a blanket off the bed when he noticed a pair of gloves on the dresser. "Has he worn these?"

"I think so," the caregiver said. "It was cold yesterday and I think he had them on."

Bryce used his own gloved hand to pick up the subject's gloves and was surprised at what he found underneath. "What's that?" he asked.

The caregiver's shoulders slumped immediately. "Um, apparently his bong."

Bryce was immediately on guard. "I don't know many two-year olds who smoke dope." He allowed a smidgen of irritation to show in his voice.

"It's why he's here, out in the sticks," the caregiver admitted. "His family said he kept sneaking onto the Seattle ferry to go downtown and do drugs with his buddies. They just couldn't handle him anymore."

"Did you share that little tidbit with the deputy?" he asked.

"No, we're so far from the ferry terminal I never thought it was an option. I guess I should have. Will you still look for him?"

"Of course," Bryce said, bouncing back to politeness. "We don't care why he's missing. This just gives us some other angles to work."

Bryce took the gloves, bagged them each separately, and then placed sterile gauze pads in each bag. When it came time to search, his teammates would scent their dogs off the gauze pads, preserving the gloves for future use.

After finding nothing else of value as a scent item, Bryce went outside to chat with the deputy.

"We found his bong. I didn't see any dope that you'd have to seize, but maybe he's off on a shopping trip."

The deputy's jaw dropped. "The guy's supposed to have the mentality of a two-year old..."

"My question too," Bryce said. "The lady says that's why he's here. He used to split from his mom's place and go over to Seattle."

"Nice work, man," the deputy said. "I knew leaving you alone with her was a good decision. We'll let the ferries know to watch for him. You still wanna deploy Sierra?"

"Sure, but I'll leave the scent articles for the trailing dogs," Bryce said. "There's a huge clear cut out back. We need to rule that area out in case he's not on a buying trip."

The deputy concurred. "Sounds good, need a second person?"

Bryce let the deputy know he'd be okay alone, and got Sierra ready to go. Without a scent article she'd be searching for any human that might be out in the woods. If they found a jogger or hiker, they'd treat them as a witness, quiz them, and go back to work.

With Sierra's vest and GPS collar in place, he gave her the magic words, "Go find," that told her they were looking for someone alive. Although it was possible their subject was deceased, it would be recent enough that live scent would be present for Sierra to detect.

Their first pass through the woods paralleled the road into the foster home. For safety, Bryce wanted to start adjacent to the road, and work a grid pattern away from it. If they searched toward a road, there was always the risk of Sierra getting ahead of him and getting hit.

Bryce saw that Sierra was in scent almost immediately. She'd hooked back toward the road they were leaving, which always made him nervous. But he let her go anyway, and eventually discovered her making circles around an abandoned cabin. There was clearly fresh scent.

"Hellooo! Anybody in therrre?" Bryce called. Looking from the outside, the place was a complete dump. Every window was broken, the roof had partially collapsed, and the main door was only partway shut. Sierra was standing with her nose next to the doorjamb.

"Base, Dog 44," was Bryce's radio call.

"Dog 44, Base. Go ahead."

"We've found an abandoned cabin and Sierra's got major interest. Nobody's answering when I yell, so we're going to look inside. It's almost due north of the residence by a couple hundred yards."

"Okay, 44. Keep us posted and for sure let us know when you're clear of the place. By the way, the trailing dogs have arrived and are just getting launched."

"44, copied. Let me know if they do or don't get a good trail out the road. That'll tell us whether he's likely back here or not."

"Received...Base clear."

Bryce pushed the door of the cabin a little further open. "Okay, girl, go on in."

Sierra went in with Bryce right behind. He quickly called her to a stop. "Sierra! Stay!" The floor was littered with broken glass and needles. It was obvious the place was what old timers would have called a shooting gallery. Probably every doper in the neighborhood went there to smoke, snort or shoot up their drug of choice.

Bryce realized his thick-soled boots would be the only safe way to search, but he could do that visually with no problem. He took Sierra outside, put her in a down-stay, and went back in. It took less than five minutes to check every nook and cranny that could have held a full-size human, and found no one.

"Base, Dog 44. The cabin is clear now, but somebody's been here recently. Let the deputy know there's a ton of drug paraphernalia here."

"This is Base, we copy. So you know, the trailing dogs seem kinda stumped. We're hearing the subject may have walked the road out and back a couple of times yesterday just for exercise. They're going to move out onto the main highway and see if they can pick up a trail actually leaving the neighborhood."

"44 copies. We'll continue searching this area then, at least until they get a solid trail going elsewhere."

"Base clear."

Bryce and Sierra continued to the end of the wooded patch, and noticed a house at the far north end of the clear cut. The developed area would become their search boundary. Bryce took Sierra to the east about 300 feet, and then turned south for another pass through the clear cut. That pass was uneventful, so Bryce shifted his grid east another 300 feet, and spun around to head back north.

Sierra immediately moved out ahead of him, much further than she'd been before. Bryce wondered if they were onto something.

As they moved north, Bryce saw Sierra go up and over a little embankment. He hurried to the top, and saw the end of a logging road beneath him. On the other side of the road was an identical embankment, obviously heaped up when a bulldozer had carved out the road.

By the time Bryce got down to the road itself, Sierra was out of sight over the other side. That's when he heard it.

A bark, followed by a low growl. It was Sierra, but Sierra never growled. She'd occasionally bark with excitement, but barking and growling were not her style.

What he saw next was even more troubling. Sierra was backing up over the top of the berm, her tail straight up and not moving. Her head was low, and locked on whatever was on the other side. A low growl continued from her throat.

"C'mere, girl," Bryce called, in as light a voice as he could muster. He didn't want his own reaction to magnify Sierra's mood. "Whatcha got?"

Sierra came back to him, but continued glancing toward the top of the berm. It was clear that whatever was on the other side had spooked her in a big way.

The options were many. A bear or coyote were first on Bryce's list, but something more sinister popped into his head. Was their subject on the other side, dead and disfigured in some disturbing way? Was Sierra reacting to seeing a human form with their head shot off, or hanging from a noose in a tree? No one suspects suicide when a subject has the mental capacity of a two-year old, but nobody had suspected drugs, either.

Bryce steeled himself for something grotesque, and made a mental note to get out of the scene if he needed to vomit. Detectives hate it when someone vomits in their crime scene. Bryce put Sierra in a stay and started over the berm, and found himself rewarded with what had to be the most unusual thing he'd ever discovered on a search.

His first guess of a bear had actually been close. Only this was a teddy bear. A teddy bear in a high chair. A teddy bear in a high chair, surrounded by other teddy bears, all in a clear cut in the middle of nowhere. The two of them had clearly stumbled into some child's fantasy picnic, with teddy bears as the permanent guests of honor.

"It's okay, Sierra. C'mon over," he called. Sierra came to the top of the berm, lowered her head, and resumed growling.

"They're just toys," he said. Bryce took the big teddy bear and shook it. Sierra stepped forward a bit, down the side of the berm. Her tail went from straight up to a short, stiff wag. She walked up to one of the bears on the ground and nudged it with her nose.

"See...just toys," Bryce told her. But his brain went back to business. Could this be some kind of retreat for their subject, a place in the woods to get away? He'd have to ask carefully, lest he doom himself to years of teasing by his colleagues.

"Base, 44," was the radio call.

"44, Base. Go ahead."

"44, um, do we know if our subject has, um, any affinity for stuffed animals?" He was not about to say "teddy bear picnic" over the radio.

"Base, 44. I'll ask. Whatcha got?"

"Just a little collection of stuffed animals, staged, sort of. They look like they've been out here longer than our subject's been living here, but we still should check."

"Stand by."

44, standing by."

Bryce's next thought was that the subject might really be nearby, stuffed animals or not. What if Sierra was honing in on his scent before being distracted by the bears? It would be embarrassing beyond belief to attribute Sierra's alert to the bears and miss a subject only a few feet away. He walked the area thoroughly to make sure no one was there.

"44, Base. No known interest in stuffed animals. Must belong to some neighborhood kids."

"Okay, 44 copies. We've marked this on the GPS and will resume searching."

Bryce and Sierra continued their sweep north, headed toward the house they'd seen earlier. If the house had a fence, he'd work right up to it. He'd known missing people to move well through the woods, only to stop and sit down at the slightest of obstacles. He didn't want to miss a subject only a few feet outside a fenced yard.

The house provided the solution to at least one mystery—the source of the teddy bears. The yard was full of children's toys, and a step-ladder had been rigged over the back fence. The kids clearly had a way into the clear cut, and Bryce imagined they would bring imaginary tea or lemonade to share with their teddy bear buddies.

The radio crackled. *"44, Base."*

"44, go ahead."

"Just as the trailing dogs were indeed getting a trail out at the highway, the local mailman stopped by. He'd seen the guy early this morning hoofing it toward town. He had no reason to think anything was amiss until he saw our poster at the mini-mart."

"44, sounds like the trailing dogs are right. How long ago was he spotted?"

"About six hours. We're going to send a dog back to where the mailman says he was and try and pick up the scent from there."

"44, okay. We're almost done with this clear cut, and on the off-chance the mailman's wrong I'd like to finish up."

"Good idea. Let us know when you're done."

Bryce and Sierra continued searching the clear cut, and as expected found nothing. The trailing dogs were too far away for Bryce's radio to pick them up, but he could hear Base's half of the conversations. It was clear that, along with the dogs, they'd sent mobile units to simply drive around the area. If the mailman had spotted him, a searcher in a truck might too.

"73, we copy. You got a direction?" was all Bryce could hear.

"73, Base again. The deputy says do not chase him. If he's in the woods we'll get another dog down there to search." Bryce was a bit confused, but experience told him the likely scenario. The mobile searchers had made contact with the guy, and he'd split.

That happened from time to time, and was always a dilemma. Bryce's radio crackled again.

"44, Base, not sure how much you're copying. 73 spotted our subject and made contact, and the guy ran off into the woods. We'd like to get you and Sierra down there to find him,"

Bryce was decidedly against foot pursuits of missing subjects. First, missing subjects aren't criminals. The fellow was under no obligation to talk to SAR personnel or anyone else, and it wasn't a crime to run into the woods. The bigger concern was that if the subject's running, what's he running toward? Every part of Kitsap County had swamps, and would be easy to bust through bushes and find oneself in four feet of water.

Bryce decided not to argue over the radio, but would chat with the deputy before deploying. He'd take his time getting back to base, and maybe the situation would resolve without him.

"Base, 44. We're on the opposite side of the clear cut, and it's going to take us awhile to get back to the truck. I take it the brush down there is too thick for the trailing dogs to follow?"

"That's right, 44. 73 reports that a dog on a long-line wouldn't get 10 feet without tangling."

"44, okay. We'll be there quick as we can. How about setting up some containment though? Let's limit the area we have to search."

"Yes, 44, we've thought of that," Base replied, sounding somewhat annoyed. *"73 and the trailing dogs are setting up in case he pops back onto the road. Also, the map says there's really nothing he could get into if he goes the other way. The whole area butts up against the base of Gold Mountain."*

Bryce didn't buy that, but held his resolve against arguing over the radio.

"44, copied. On the way."

It didn't take long for the containment suggestion to pay off.

"38, Base copies. Is he going to let you give him a ride home this time?" was all Bryce could hear. His radio crackled again. *"Okay, well if a dog is what it takes, then he can ride with them. What's your ETA back here?"*

Bryce couldn't hear the answer, but the next call was for him.

"44, Base."

"44, go ahead."

"Yeah, when the subject saw one of the dogs he melted. He wouldn't talk to 73, but came right out of the woods to play with 38's dog. He's going to ride back with her and the bloodhound."

"44, whatever works. We've got about another ten minutes weaving our way out of this clear cut, so I imagine we'll all arrive together."

Bryce got back to base to find not only the rest of his team and the now found subject, but Bob Wright as well.

"Hey, Bob, what brings you by?" Bryce asked.

"We've had so many of these searches end up as suspicious deaths that I thought I'd get a head start," Wright answered. "Looks like this one turned out okay."

"Yeah, for once," Bryce said. "It's been a goofy one though. First they tell us the guy has the mentality of a two-year old, but I find his bong. Then we get out in the woods and we find a bunch of teddy bears arrayed like they were having a picnic. Scared the doggie-poop out of Sierra."

"That's kinda weird. We don't need any more weird right now," Wright said. "These other cases are starting to keep me up at night."

"How's Lorraine doing on that hit-and-run car we found?" Bryce asked. "I mean, if you're allowed to tell me."

"I have no problem telling you anything, Wright responded. "Hell, you could probably do a better job than one particular detective I'm thinking of..."

"Would that be Detective Hicks?" Bryce asked quietly.

"Oh, you noticed? He's not our best and brightest, and I'm sorry he's taking it out on you."

"No worries, though he does insist that I call you 'Sergeant Wright' when he's around."

"You can call me Bob anytime. Look, if there's anything you've noticed at these scenes I wanna hear it. I've got Hicks slicing and dicing the backgrounds of our victims and he's coming up with squat. He's looked for anything they might have in common. Going through divorces...military..."

"They're all guys," Bryce said. Wright never heard him.

"Did they molest somebody...do they gamble..."

"Bob...sir...they're all *guys*," Bryce stressed. "All I can tell you is that we normally get a mix of search assignments. It'll be a ten-year old autistic kid one week, and an Alzheimer's patient the next. These cases have all been bing-bing-bing, adult males in otherwise good health who suffer unexplainable deaths. Even the suicide seemed a little odd."

"Aw jeez." Wright was clearly frustrated. "Hicks has a spreadsheet a mile wide with everything but their shoe sizes and we never paid attention to that column. "

"All that's your deal, sir," Bryce said. "I just work the scenes with my dog."

"Yeah, I heard Hicks said that to you," Wright said, smiling. "Don't listen to him. But do check on whether his legs are still cramping from his day at the gym. I think he got the message."

"Message?" Bryce asked. "And I never really understood that 'wilderness gym' thing."

"Two people on a body bag just sucks…like…worse than anything a personal trainer will do to you. I feel bad for the deputy coroner who had to help carry, but I think it's lesson learned. Detective Hicks will be more appreciative of you folks, at least until he's able to walk upright again.

"Thanks, sir. I'll let Katie know."

Chapter Thirteen

Autopsy

"So, Waylon, show me whatcha got."

Elroy Patterson was entering his third term as the elected Sheriff, but had been with the department his whole adult life. He knew Waylon Hicks was a knucklehead, but had promoted him to detective anyway.

Patterson had seen unremarkable employees become stars when given the *right* job. He believed it was his role to put people in positions where their weaknesses could become strengths.

Oddly enough, he hadn't learned that in the Sheriff's Office. He learned it when he took on the job of assistant coach for his son's little league team. The senior coach put the slowest kid on the team at catcher—because he wouldn't have to run much. A player who would have been mediocre at any other position started studying opposing batters and working on his throw to second base. That catcher was Patterson's eldest boy, who wound up leveraging baseball into a career as a successful stockbroker. He'd gotten a full-ride athletic scholarship at a prestigious college solely because a little league coach knew how to line up peoples' strengths and weaknesses.

But the same magic hadn't occurred in Hicks' career as a detective—at least not so far. The kindly Sheriff knew that some of his command staff wanted Detective Hicks booted back to uniform patrol, maybe booted out of the department entirely. He knew it might come to that someday. But while some leaders throw rope to struggling employees, Patterson took the opposing path. He'd give marginal employees every possible chance to succeed. That way, if he did have to fire or demote them, he could do so with a clear conscience.

His failsafe was Bob Wright. He knew that with Wright as Hicks' supervisor, no case would truly suffer from Hicks' failings.

Hicks looked around the Sheriff's conference table. Also present were the undersheriff, Wright and Hicks' peer detective Lenora Hogan. All were staring at him expectantly.

"Well, I've got a lot of data but not a lot of results," was Hicks' opening statement. "I gathered all the data I was *told* to gather, but as I expected it meant nothing."

Patterson couldn't believe his ears. This substandard detective was trying to throw his supervisor under the bus in front of the department's leadership. He said nothing, but noticed that Bob Wright's ears turned an uncommon shade of crimson.

Hicks had at least prepared copies of his spreadsheet for everyone, showing the myriad of characteristics he'd compiled about the victims. The names were down the side, with various traits across the top. The columns ranged from straightforward age and race, to employment, schooling and prior military. On the far right, the spreadsheet got a little more personal. It included whether the person gambled, cheated on their spouse, or was known to smoke a little dope.

"We were supposed to look for commonalities," Hicks continued. "There just aren't any, this was a complete waste of time. These accidental deaths are just what they first seemed…accidental."

Wright was the first to speak. His ears were back to their normal color, and he spoke in measured tones. "The first commonality is that they're all dead, in numbers we haven't ever seen in this county. You've done a great job on this spreadsheet, Waylon, but there's gotta be something we're all missing here."

The Sheriff continued to study the spreadsheet, and eventually raised a question. "What's this column labelled 'BenMot?'"

"That's Beneficiary Motive," Hicks replied. "It's whether their loved ones had any insurance motive to kill them."

"I don't see a lot of X's in those boxes," Patterson said.

"That's right, you don't." Hicks was starting to sound defensive. "Some of the dead guys had insurance, of course. But nobody had enough to make their spouse want to kill them."

It was the undersheriff's turn to speak. "How do you know that?"

"First, because of couple of the widows are going to lose their houses," Hicks explained. "But there's an even better way. The insurance industry is always looking to avoid fraud, so the companies have all joined this database. They want to make sure somebody's not loaded up with multiple policies from multiple companies, way beyond their personal worth. The companies also track benefits paid, and the payouts for all of our supposed victims were completely within normal ranges."

"Okay, next question," the Sheriff continued. "I don't see it on the spreadsheet, but did you look for any direct connections between our victims? Maybe a trait you wouldn't otherwise have tracked but turns out to be something common to all of them."

"What, like a bowling league or the same church?" Hicks was showing every sign of being defensive. "How am I supposed to figure that out?"

"The last two weeks of their lives is how you figure that out," Wright interjected. "Reconstruct the last two weeks of their lives and see if any of them cross paths."

"That'll mean talking to the widows and loved ones, making them go through it all over again." Hicks had never been sensitive to victims, so the Sheriff assumed he was dodging work again.

Lenora Hogan had been silent up till that point. "I can help. We can quickly interview the wives and get some kind of timeline for each of them. If it's church or a bowling league, it'll pop out pretty quickly."

The Sheriff knew Hogan as what old-timers called a "silver tongued devil." That's a cop who can talk to anybody, from any walk of life and in any horrible situation. That's why he'd made her a hostage negotiator, and she'd proved her skill many times over.

"It'll take at least a couple weeks," Hicks objected. "Even with two of us."

"Then it'll take two weeks," Wright jumped in, his patience with Hicks just about gone. "I'll expect those timelines two weeks from today."

"Well, that gives me 13 days," Hicks argued. "Because I'm losing the rest of today to an autopsy. Remember, you've got me going to those as well."

"What autopsy?" the Sheriff said. "We haven't had any new deaths."

"It was a hospital death," Hicks said. "The ER doc thought something looked amiss, so he asked the coroner to have a look."

Wright's voice got a touch louder. "And you were going to tell me this...when? I mean if the ER doc thought it was suspicious then we oughta be in for more than just the autopsy. When and where did this guy die? Is there a scene we should be looking at?"

"I was planning to find that out at the autopsy." The lameness of his own excuse was obvious to even Hicks himself. "I'll get all the details I can, and call the ER if the coroner doesn't have something."

Wright got even louder. "No. You're going to get the guy's name and the name of the hospital and give it to Lenora. While you're at the autopsy she'll be gathering information you should already have."

"Right," was all Hicks could say. He and Lenora left the room.

"Close the door please," the Sheriff said as they left. "Bob, would you hang here a minute?"

"I'm sorry, Sheriff, I know I kinda lost it at Hicks," Wright offered as soon as the door shut.

"You're doing fine," was the Sheriff's reassuring comeback. "I know I stuck you with a clinker by promoting him. I was really hoping he'd find his niche."

"Well, he's not. He's a terrible interviewer and his reports are even worse. I have trouble getting him to do any work at all."

"I know," the Sheriff said. "The reason I gave him a chance is because you're his boss. I knew we'd be safe taking a risk with you as the backup. Are you telling me he's so bad you can't fix him?"

Wright stopped for a moment. He shook his head and said "I don't think we're to the point of demoting him, but the problem is his attitude. He doesn't seem to *want* to get better. I can work with anybody who's trying, but he's not trying."

The Sheriff had seen the issue come up before, and in some cases resolve with patience. "Let's give it a little more time," he said. "I trust you're keeping good documentation?"

Wright's answer was unequivocal. "I've got a drop-file on the guy an inch thick. I'll work with him as long as you say, but if you decide to send him back to patrol you'll have plenty of paper to justify it."

"Okay. Is there someplace in the department you think he'd do well?" The Sheriff was still trying to get his players into the right positions.

"Well he sure ain't 'Officer Friendly,' so we can't send him into schools," was Wright's first answer. "And the county council took away that position inspecting junkyards and tow companies. He'd have been great dealing with those folks. Nice doesn't work with them anyway."

"Well, let's think on it," the kindly Sheriff said. "You keep documenting but try to figure out someplace not just to stash him, but where he really might find his niche."

"Got it, boss. Thanks."

* * *

Hogan was already on the phone to the ER. In a rare stroke of luck, the attending physician was actually at work and available for a call. The receptionist offered a quick "hold please," and Dr. Mike Avery picked up on the second ring.

"Dr. Avery, my name is Lenora Hogan and I'm a detective with the Sheriff's Office. I'm trying to find out a little more about a patient you sent to our coroner's office for autopsy. That's kind of unusual."

"I know," the doctor said. "I was actually conflicted about it but there were some things I just couldn't resolve."

"Such as…?"

"From a medical perspective, we really couldn't figure out what killed him. It looked like a heart attack but not all of the right symptoms were present. We thought maybe a thrombosis, a clot, but he didn't respond to the medicine we give for that. What was really out of whack was his wife's reaction to the death."

"Okayyy?"

"I assume you've done death notifications," Avery said.

"Too many," was Hogan's truthful response.

"Well, I've been an ER doc for going on 15 years, and the wife's response just wasn't right. I've seen everything from outright fainting, to anger, disbelief, even people accusing me of botching the case. This wife was just emotionally flat. No grief, no anger, all business. She just wanted to know how to release the body to a funeral home. And here's the kicker—she wanted one that does cremations."

Hogan immediately understood the implications. "So what happened when you said the body had to go to the coroner's office?"

"I didn't at first. This seemed like every other natural death, and since it's a death attended by a doctor there's no requirement for autopsy. After I thought about it for a few minutes I changed my mind. And, full disclosure here, she didn't seem to care."

Hogan was starting to agree the wife's reaction was suspicious, at least having heard only one side of the story. "What excuse did you use for the change in procedure?" she asked.

"I just told her there was some fine print in the rules and we needed to send the remains over to the coroner. She had no objections, which actually ratchets down the concern. But I thought it was still worth checking."

"Why?"

"One of your detectives was in here a while back. I can't remember his name, but I remember thinking it was like some country western star...a singer. Same name and not very common."

"Could that have been Waylon Hicks?" Hogan asked.

"Yup. That's it. I keyed on Waylon Jennings," the doc said. "He was checking on natural deaths and didn't seem happy about it. We didn't have much to offer him."

"Well, I hope he wasn't a bother. He can be a little grumpy at times." Hogan was trying to put a good face on it.

"We get all types in here, so no bother," Avery said. "But just the fact that he was asking made me think of you guys when this came up a few days later."

Hogan wanted to confirm what she'd heard, by repeating it back. "But in this case, nothing on the medical side that raised any alarms…is that what you're saying?"

"No needle marks, and our initial tox screen was clear," Avery explained. "But we don't check for a lot of drugs in that initial treatment. We look for the common drugs that people screw up with, legal or illegal. We didn't find anything in his system that would have explained a sudden death."

"Heart attack?" Hogan was trying to cover all bases.

"It's possible but we didn't think so. By the time he got here there was no rhythm at all, so hard to say on that. He didn't respond to shocks or the drugs we gave him, and usually you get something—a fibrillation maybe."

"What was his overall health…his appearance at least?"

"Looked like he worked out," Avery said. "But he didn't have the massive muscles of somebody who uses steroids, and again, no needle marks."

Hogan got contact information for the widow, and thanked the doctor for his vigilance. She knew her next call would be more difficult, but she decided to get it over with. Maybe she'd go two-for-two, finding people on the first try. It was not to be, and she left a message.

* * *

Hicks hated autopsies, but not quite so much since the coroner got his new office. He still had to watch, but he did so from an observation room adjacent to the operatory. That meant he didn't have to smell anything, at least. Ventilation in the new facility was excellent, and being in a separate room meant he also didn't have to listen to the sound of the saw used to open up flesh and bone.

"Everything's normal, which isn't normal," the pathologist said over the intercom. Dr. Peter Jamieson was a contract pathologist on retainer to the coroner's office. "I agree with the ER doc. There's no reason for this guy to have just keeled over."

Hicks pressed the button on his end to respond. "Any needle marks? Maybe a poison the lab didn't know to look for."

"Not a mark. This guy was in great shape and still is. His heart looks good and I'm still running his major arteries but I'm not finding any plaque or anything that would lead to a clot."

At that point even Hicks was starting to suspect they were on to something. The human body is easy to kill, but it's a pretty decent machine and doesn't generally just up and die for no reason.

"Wait a minute," the pathologist said. "His aorta feels mushy."

Hicks pushed his button again. "Clot?"

"No, different feel. I gotta open this up and see if it's what I suspect."

Hicks waited silently on his side of the window as the pathologist went to work with a scalpel. From his angle, Hicks couldn't see inside the chest, but clearly some knife-work was going on.

"Well, there ya go," the pathologist said, a tone of relief in his voice.

"Wanna share?" Hicks asked.

"It's a one-in-a-million congenital aortic dissection. Dissections happen all the time, but usually after somebody's been in a crash and hit their chest on the steering wheel."

"He wasn't in a crash," Hicks reminded the doc.

"And this isn't that kind of dissection…that's not really even the right word," Jamieson said. "Think of delamination. Kind of like when you peel the paper backing of some sticky tape. The inside layer of his aorta just came loose, and formed a check valve."

Now Hicks was really confused. "A check-valve? You mean like in my water pipes?"

"Exactly right," Jamieson said. In this case, a layer of his aorta peeled off inside and flapped shut. His heart couldn't pump against it and his body just shut down."

"Isn't that just a heart attack?" Hicks asked.

"It's different than a clot. There's no pain, no clutching of the chest or trouble breathing. The patient just quietly goes unconscious and death follows pretty quickly."

"So…natural death?" Hicks knew he'd be grilled six ways from Sunday, and wanted to have all the answers. "No way to trigger this with drugs or a blow to the chest?"

"None at all." The doc was firm. "A blow to the chest would have left a bruise, and he'd have passed out pretty soon after. This is an obvious natural death, but nothing the ER missed. Only about one percent of those who get this are saved. If you're gonna survive this one, you pretty much need to be in the ER when it hits."

Hicks was already packing his stuff. A better detective would have gone into the operatory and had the doctor show him the artery and the flap. But Hicks was Hicks. At the words "natural death" he'd checked out intellectually, and was quickly checking out physically.

* * *

"Detective Hogan, please," the voice on the phone said.

"Speaking." Hogan was getting ready to leave for the day, but dinner had been late before and if this was who she thought it was, dinner would be late again.

"I'm Betty Taylor. I got a message to call you. You said it was about my husband."

"Yes, Ms. Taylor. Thanks for returning my call," Hogan replied, turning on the charm. She'd treat Taylor like the grieving widow until she had a concrete reason to do otherwise. "Are you doing okay? I'm really sorry for the loss of your husband."

"I'm doing fine. I'm just grateful we don't have any children. I'll get through this and move on."

Now it was Hogan's turn go on alert. Not red alert yet, but maybe bright yellow. One thing widows almost universally say is that they don't know how they're going to get through life. Three sentences into their conversation, Betty Taylor was justifying the ER doc's intuition.

"I'm glad you're doing well," Hogan sympathized. "I need to talk to you about your husband's last couple of weeks. They're doing the autopsy now but it generally never tells the full story."

"I have to say I don't know much about his last two weeks. We were living in different parts of the house and were headed to a split," Taylor said.

"I'm sorry to hear that," Hogan replied, her tone not matching her increased level of interest. "Were you planning on a divorce?"

142

"It was looking that way," the widow Taylor replied. "Jason was clinically depressed, but I just couldn't help him and couldn't tolerate his moods any longer. He'd lost his job and all his benefits, and he didn't seem to appreciate all the work I did to support us."

"Does losing his job mean he's lost all his insurance?" Hogan was the best at sounding concerned while letting criminals talk themselves into prison. "Are you going to get anything to help you get by?"

"Probably not a dime. His insurance lapsed when he got fired. It's okay. I wouldn't have gotten anything if we'd split and we were losing the house anyway. If our equity covers the closing costs I'll be happy."

"I'm so sorry," Hogan said, her mood shifting to genuine concern. But she still had a job to do. "Ms. Taylor, I still need to ask you some questions. Anytime we have an unexplained death we reconstruct the victim's previous two weeks. Sometimes the answer is there, rather than from the autopsy.

"I'd like to help, but we just weren't connecting. He used to work out, and had been in great shape. We'd go for runs together, come home, and fix dinner for each other. Since he got depressed, he spent all his time in the guest room playing video games. He'd sleep there too...hadn't so much as kissed me in six months. The only thing that changed when he got fired was that he could play video games 24/7."

Hogan made a mental note to limit her son's time on the computer, and pressed on. "Ma'am, we've had a series of unexplained deaths in the county, and we're trying hard to see if there's any connection. Had your husband been sick?"

"Physically, no. Mentally, I already said he was depressed," Taylor answered. "I started to wonder if he'd taken pills or something, and then I realized I just didn't care."

"He *was* your husband…" was Logan's reply. "You must have felt something."

"Nope. My give-a-damn's busted. I'd feel bad for his parents if they were still alive. He was an only child, so no siblings. And like I said, thank God we didn't have any children. You probably think I'm some kind of witch, but it was over. I don't feel any more pain than if he'd been a complete stranger, collapsing on the sidewalk in front of me."

"That explains the ER doc's intuition," Hogan thought to herself. She'd owe him a phone call to let him know his senses were working. Maybe that would pay off in a future case, one that really was a homicide.

"Okay," Hogan started to wrap up. "But his last two weeks, really nothing but the basement and video games? No bowling, or fishing? He didn't have any other activities."

Taylor was ready to end the conversation as well. "That's the thing about depression. When he was in the deepest part, nothing made him happy. He'd shut everything and everyone out— including me. No, he didn't catch the flu at the bowling alley, or get an infection from a fishhook. Whatever killed him was within him. I'm afraid I can't add anything more."

"I'm so sorry," Hogan replied, sincerely now. "Can I just ask one thing? In case there's some oddball disease out there, can you sign a release for his previous medical records?"

"I suppose," Taylor said. "There's probably a boatload of paperwork. He'd been going to one doc after another for his depression. Can you just e-mail it over? I'll sign and scan it, and send it back."

Hogan allowed as that would suffice, and wrapped up the conversation. Just as she did so, Hicks returned from the coroner's office, with a look of satisfaction on his face.

"Doc said it's a natural, no way to fake this one," he offered cheerfully. "His aorta came apart on the inside and blocked things up like a heart attack. But it wasn't a clot, which is why their usual treatments didn't work. It's a pretty rare event, and doc says the only way to survive is to actually be in the ER when it hits."

It annoyed Hogan that Hicks was right. It happened so seldom, it was actually hard to believe. But what she'd heard from the widow jibed with what Hicks had found, so she'd let it go.

"I'm going to tell our illustrious boss," Hicks said, not stopping at his desk.

"You're gloating too much," was Hogan's warning. "You better let me tell him. He's not going to hit me. Did you see his face when we were in with the Sheriff?"

"No, what?" Hick really was clueless.

"Jeez, you dissed him in front of his own boss. You talked about this assignment being a 'waste of time.' That's not something you say to your boss's boss."

"Look, if you want to tell him, fine," Hicks barked back. "I'm just dropping off this paperwork and I'm outta here."

"Um, yeah. I think it's best if I handle this," Hogan said, immediately kicking herself. She realized too late that if she'd let Hicks tick off the boss again, she might be rid of him. "See you tomorrow."

Chapter Fourteen
Warrant Wagon

It was the classic kind of rattletrap rig that cops everywhere know will run up their arrest stats. If nothing else, there will be mechanical violations they can put down as a contact-and-warning. But this car was filled to the brim with what can only be described as "crap." Almost always some of that crap is stolen, and more often than not there are drugs hidden underneath.

"Good evening, sir. I stopped you tonight because you have a headlight out. I couldn't tell if you were a car or a motorcycle coming at me." Jason Link was an experienced deputy, and he'd decided that quickly telling the person why they'd been stopped lessened the number of arguments.

"Aw jeez, I thought I had that fixed," was the driver's nervous response. "It's the right one, right?"

"So you knew it was a problem…" Link was throwing rope.

"I thought it was a *fixed* problem, man. Like…I'm sorry…I'll go home and work on it some more."

Link went ahead with the next step in the process. "Okay, we'll make the headlight a warning. But I do need your driver's license, registration and proof of insurance."

"What for? If you're gonna warn me, warn me. I'll go home and fix the damn thing!"

Link remained professional, and not just for the dash-cam. He was still throwing rope. "I still need to ID you sir, and make sure the car is yours and properly insured."

"Well screw you. I don't have any ID so you might as well just take me to jail for the headlight."

"Well, we don't need to go there yet," Link replied coolly. "Do you have anything with your name on it?"

"My wallet's at home."

"All this stuff in the car, and there's nothing here with your name on it?" More rope. "Not a receipt...repair slip...electric bill?"

"Nope." Wrong answer.

"Okay, then what's your name and birthday?" Some slack in the line.

"Bill Creighton...9-21-92." The driver rattled it off like he had experience. "Want my shirt size, too?"

"No, Bill, I just want to get through this contact so you can get that headlight fixed. I need you to work with me here." Link's tactic now was to make small talk and buy some time. "The headlight's dangerous, man. People can't tell if you're a motorcycle or a car over the center line. They don't know if they're gonna get drilled by a drunk. I know it seems like I'm being chicken, but that's a violation that messes with other drivers."

"Okay, okay, I get it. What more do you want from me? I'll go home and get it fixed." The driver was becoming more agitated, and starting to sweat.

"Is Bill or William?" Link asked, ignoring the anger.

"Jeez, it's William."

"Have you got a middle initial?" Link was tightening the line, gently.

The driver paused and finally answered…"J."

Link set the hook, hard. He'd done some quick math. "Okay, Bill. How old are you?"

"What? I told you my birthdate." Link could almost see the wheels turning in the driver's head.

"It's a simple question, Bill. How old are you?"

"…Twenty…seven."

"Wrong answer, my friend," Link said, reaching for the door handle. "You're lying about your birth date and probably your name, too. I need you to come on back to my car while we talk some more."

"Bill" got out of the car and started to look around. Link saw the body language of fight-or-flight, and reacted immediately. Bill found himself spun hard and pushed against the car. Link spoke boilerplate language, right out of the Supreme Court opinion. "You're not under arrest, but you're not free to leave. I'm handcuffing you for my safety and yours."

"Yeah...yeah. Y'know, I've always wondered what the concern was with MY safety?" was sarcastic response.

"Keeps me from shooting you if you twitch wrong," Link said, without a hint of emotion.

Bill, or whatever his name was, had no response.

Link continued. "Now, what's your name and date of birth?"

"Bill...William...Wilson. Middle is really J. And my birthday is Sept. 21, but it's in 94."

"Thanks, Bill. You've admitted giving me false info, so now you *are* under arrest. We're gonna head downtown and put you on a fingerprint machine. That'll tell me for sure who you are. What's goin' on, are you suspended?"

"Nope, the judge gave me my license back last month. I paid the fees and everything."

Link checked off on the next reason people lie. "Do you have warrants?"

"Nope, I took care of everything, just like I told that search guy the other night."

"What 'search guy?'" Link asked.

"The one with the dog. When I was up the tree. He asked if I had warrants and I told him no."

Link knew there'd been a SAR mission a few nights' previous, and the locker room laughter was that the subject had been found up a tree. The coincidence of meeting the man a few days later took Link by surprise.

"Well, we'll check and make sure there are no warrants. If not, you'll probably be recog'd from jail as soon as the fingerprints confirm your identity," Link said. He liked dangling a quick release in front of arrestees. It helped keep them from fighting. "What do you want to do with the car?"

"What?"

"The car...you know...the one that started all this...with the headlight out. You're not legally parked here where you pulled over, and I don't have time to wait for somebody to come get it. I'm calling a tow and need to know if you have anything valuable in the car."

"Um, no, nothing."

"Really? It's stacked to the brim with all kinds of stuff, and probably the wallet you didn't want to give up." Link wanted to make sure the man claiming he was Bill Wilson wouldn't later claim the tow company had stolen his Rolex watch. "There's gotta be something in the car you care about."

"No, it's okay. How much will it cost me if you tow it?"

"I dunno. Depends on how quickly you get it from them, but with even a few hours' storage it'll probably be a couple hundred bucks."

"Aw, man...do you really have to do this?"

Link ignored the remark, and decided to do a cursory inventory anyway. He'd take a few pictures just to cover his backside, but would stop short of what might be deemed an illegal search. His plan was to document what could be seen from the outside, and note Wilson's statement that there was nothing of value in the car. The game changed, though, with his first real look inside the car.

"Hey Bill, is there anything illegal in the car I need to know about?"

Bill's answer reflected his years as a meth addict. "That's your way of asking me if there are drugs in the car. No, not that I know of."

Link was on the hook now. If he asked any more questions to somebody in handcuffs, he needed to read them their Miranda rights. But if he read Wilson those rights, he was sure the savvy crook would clam up. He left the handcuffed man leaning against his police cruiser, and went back to Wilson's car for a better look.

It was undeniable. Poking from under the passenger seat Link could see the corner of a plastic bag, with a white powder inside. What he also hadn't seen from the driver's side was a small glass pipe in the passenger side cup holder. He now had legal reason to search the car, even though that meant a warrant. It was time to go back and chat with Bill.

"Look, I can see your drugs from the passenger window, and your pipe too. So instead of a tow lot, your car is headed for the Sheriff's Office. You won't get it back until we have a warrant, and you'll likely sit in jail until we've finished searching it."

"Look man, I don't know nothing about no drugs." Wilson was starting to panic. "I had a friend in the car yesterday and those must be his."

"Riiiight," Link replied, not trying to hide his skepticism. "The drugs always belong to somebody else. Well, you can forget about getting recog'd tonight. You're staying in jail at least till we get the drugs out of your car and get you formally charged. Look, we're far enough down the road I need to read you your rights."

"I know 'em," Wilson responded. He'd heard them so many times, even his drug-addled mind could probably have recited them by heart. Link went ahead anyway, finishing with the obligatory "having these rights in mind, do you now wish to speak to me?"

"Um, maybe," Wilson hesitated. "What if I knew something about somebody? Would that help my case?"

"Depends on what you know, and who the somebody is," Link shot back. "Better be a bigger fish than you and your baggie of meth."

Wilson looked Link directly in the eye and never hesitated. "It's not about drugs at all. It's just like I told that kid with the dog: a guy tried to get me to kill somebody."

"Really?" Link asked. "You know, meth makes you paranoid."

"I handle my paranoia really well, man. That's why I was up the tree. When I get like that I just get away from everybody. I might be hooked on meth, but I know damn well what it does to you. I'm not killing anybody for meth, and I'm not killing anybody for money, either. I told the guy no."

Link was starting to think he should call a detective, but he didn't want to sound the alarm too quickly because of a desperate, drug addicted nutbag. "So who was this somebody who wanted somebody else killed?"

"I don't know." Wilson started fidgeting and sweating as he spoke. Part of that was the meth, but to Link, part of it looked like legitimate fear. "He started showing up at this bar I hang at. We played a couple games of pool and got to talking…wait a minute. Is this gonna help me or not?"

Link was clear. "I don't make promises I can't keep. But for now, we'll skip booking you into jail and take you to the office instead. There's a detective I want you to talk with."

"You still gotta tow my car?" was Wilson's next question.

Link wasn't above a little wheeling and dealing. "If you give me permission to move it, and permission to take your dope, I'll park it legally over there. If what you say pans out, not only will I not arrest you, but I'll personally bring you back here so you can pick up your car—minus the drugs, of course."

Wilson showed he could deal with the best of 'em. "You're gonna get the stuff anyway...so yeah. Move the car and take the dope. Your detective will like what I have to say."

* * *

"Hey Bob...it's Jason Link. Sorry about the late call."

Wright was in bed, hoping to get a good night's sleep. Second best, he thought, was a call that would make it worth being awakened.

"Hey yourself. What's up?"

"I got a guy in custody, false info and possession, but he says somebody tried to hire him to run somebody down. Don't you have an unsolved hit and run from a few weeks back?"

"Yeah, it's Lenora Hogan's case, but she's off for a few days with a sick kid. The guy willing to talk?"

"Yup. If he gives you something good I promised to skip the charges and take him back to his car. You wanna meet us at the office?"

"Can you book him and I'll talk to him at the jail in the morning?" Wright really didn't want to get out of bed.

"That wasn't the deal," Link pressed. "If I book him he'll think I've gone back on our agreement. And if he gets some time to think about this he might get cold feet."

"You're right. But I had to ask. See you in 30."

* * *

Link had left Wilson in an interview room, and moved the handcuffs to the front. It was marginally more comfortable than being handcuffed behind the back, but still limited Wilson's ability to get violent. Meth addicts can go ballistic for any reason, or no reason. Link was willing to take a small chance, but only a small one.

"Hi Bob. Sorry again to get you out of bed. But I really thought...."

Wright interrupted Link. "You thought absolutely right. We need to hit this guy right now while he's feeling the heat. Which room?"

"Interview A. I handcuffed him in front as a goodwill gesture. I also got him a soda so hopefully he's feeling the love."

"That's nice, but if he doesn't we're gonna make him feel the heat," Wright said. "You care to join us?"

"Can I?" Link was indeed grateful. "I'm planning to take the detective test this fall."

"Don't think I'm being nice. You've got the relationship with Mr....um...Wilson. I want you there to make nice with him. I have to ask the hard questions, so you're the good cop to my bad cop, okay?"

The two men entered the room. Link sat across the square table from Wilson, with Wright sitting to the side. Many interviewers believe putting the table between the subject and interviewer creates a barrier. Conversely, by sitting "just around the corner" from Wilson, Wright could sidle up and invade his personal space if need be. But first, Wright made sure of the preliminaries.

"Bill, I'm Bob Wright, and I'm here to talk with you about that matter you mentioned to Deputy Link. You're here as a witness, and Link has already read you your rights about the dope and stuff. We won't use anything you say here in that case and just like you, we're hoping it goes away. I really hope you have some information that will justify us forgetting all about that."

Wilson was becoming more comfortable about diming somebody out. "Man, I'll tell you anything you want to know. I just don't know much."

"Well, the deal is you tell us every damned thing you know, and we'll give you credit for good faith," Wright said. "Lie once and we're done and you're off to booking."

"Okay, okay. So this guy starts showing up at this bar I hang at, he doesn't look real comfortable and tries making small talk with everybody and most of us start thinking he's a cop 'cuz he just doesn't fit, then we start playing pool and he asks me about my driving record so then I'm really nervous and he wants to know if I've ever been in a wreck and how I handled it and did I freak..."

"Whoa, Bill, slow down buddy," Wright tried laughing to lighten the moment. "I want you to tell me everything, but not in one breath. I'm getting old and my brain doesn't work that fast."

"Sorry, man, but I just can't go back to jail."

"We're not looking for a reason to put you back in jail. We want this guy really bad, so you've got the power here. So long as you don't screw up with a lie, you're golden. Now, did this guy give you a name?"

"That's the weird thing," Wilson continued, still not able to slow down. "He told me his name was Jack. He told the barmaid his name was Jake. The next time he came in he told this crazy old lady who's always looking to hook up that his name was John. Now I could see giving her a fake name, and a fake phone number too…I mean she's mega-ugly and a mean drunk besides. But at least I knew he wasn't a cop because a cop woulda had a better story."

"Well, I'll give ya that," Wright said. "When I was undercover we drilled our story so well it was my real name I screwed up later."

"Riiight," Wilson said. "I mean, I've been busted by undercovers so I know this guy couldn't be."

Wright tried drilling down a bit. "So, did the barmaid card him?

"At that bar? She'd sell booze to a ten-year old if he had the cash."

"Okay, so let's move on. When did he try to get you to kill somebody?"

"Third or fourth time he's there. Like I said he starts asking me about my driving record, if I've ever been in a crash. I'm starting to think he wants to hire me for deliveries or something. Then I think he's going to hire me to deliver drugs or something and I'm like 'Okay, if the money's right.' Then he asks if I've ever seen anybody killed."

Wright had always wondered how somebody would break the ice when they wanted somebody killed. He nodded but didn't say anything.

"So like, yeah, I've seen somebody die. My friend OD'd and the medics didn't get there quick enough. And he goes, 'No, I mean killed, not just died' and I'm like 'Wow, this is getting intense but no I've never seen anybody killed' so he asks me if I think I could handle it and like sure, I mean you see videos all the time."

Wright was becoming skeptical. "So this guy you barely know and who barely knows you starts asking you about killing people. That's pretty reckless...a little hard to believe."

"Man, I wouldn't have believed it either. But he did. Then he suddenly changes the subject...I thought...and starts telling me about this dude who did him dirt. The guy screwed him out of both his business and his wife. His eyes got this weird look when he talked about him."

"What did he say?" Wright used his position at the corner to the table to lean in.

"Just that this guy had an affair with his wife, and then she wanted her half of the family business. He couldn't afford to buy her out, so he just had to give it to her I guess."

"Make sense to you?" Wright asked. He looked Wilson directly in the eye, so that his own raised eyebrows were visible.

"I dunno, man. It was none of my business anyway, the guy was just talking."

Wright honed in. "But he was 'just talking' about killing someone. Did he actually tell you how he wanted it done?"

"He had a car. He said he wanted the guy run down and I said like what if somebody gets my license plate and he said he had the perfect untraceable rig all I'd have to do was wipe down the steering wheel when I dumped it and nobody would ever trace it to either of us."

Link was watching the conversation, and figured out what poker players would call a "tell" with Wilson. When he'd been lying earlier, he'd spoken slowly, as if he had to figure out what story to tell. Now, Wilson was prattling on nonstop without time to think up a lie.

"But you didn't do it?"

"No, I chickened out. I told the guy I'd rob or steal for my meth, but killing somebody wasn't me. He got really mad and told me I'd better not tell anybody what he'd said. He said he'd kill ME if I blabbed."

Wright pressed home. "But you told that searcher guy who found you up in the tree."

"Not very much!" Wilson protested. "I thought it was the killer dude coming after me. When I found out it was actually some do-gooder I clammed back up."

"Okay," Wright said. "You hang right here for a few minutes while Jason and I go outside and talk. You need to use the can or anything?"

"No, I'm good. Thanks…I've told you everything man, and I can't go back to jail."

Wright softened his tone, but again looked Wilson in the eye. "There's always stuff people remember. I'm not accusing you of hiding anything, but memories are weird. While we're outside I want you to think of every conversation you had with the guy and every single thing he told you. And I'm going to want a description of him, right down to the last mole."

"He dyed his hair. I remember the first time I saw him he was blonde. The night he asked me to kill the dude he had black roots."

"That's good, Bill. You keep thinking like that and I'm pretty sure Deputy Link here will magically lose those drugs."

* * *

"You believe him?" was Link's first question in the hall.

"I do," Wright replied. "We put out a lot of public information about that SUV, but we didn't tell anybody it was untraceable. And not even many people inside the department know that the inside was wiped clean and I mean clean. It wasn't just prints that were smudged or unusable, it was wiped."

Link agreed. "When he was lying his ass off earlier, he talked slow and hesitated. When he was running his mouth inside just now he didn't have time to think up crap."

"What I don't get," Wright said, "was Bryce not saying anything about this. He found the car, so he knew what was going on. He's normally more on the ball than that."

"Well, that's another way to see if Wilson is telling the truth. We can check with Bryce and see what he remembers from their conversation. If he missed it, he missed it. The kid's got a great track record but we all have bad nights."

Link headed off toward the deputies' report-writing room. "I'll give him a call and let you know."

* * *

"Hey Bryce, it's Jason Link," came the phone call. "You got a minute?"

Bryce was in his room, having been sound asleep. Sierra was laying at the foot of his bed, also now awake at the sound of the phone. Groggily, Bryce answered with "Sure, what's up?"

"Well, I gotta ask you a question," Link began. "You're not in trouble or anything but it's about the other night, with the guy in the tree."

Bryce was wide awake now. As soon as someone says "you're not in trouble or anything," you're in trouble. "Is there a problem? He didn't fall out of the tree or anything did he? Is he alive?"

"He's fine," Link replied. "And you are too…really. But we've got the guy in an interview room. I popped him with some drugs and he's trying to talk his way out of it…either that or he's trying to lie his way out of it. That's where you come in."

"Okay…?"

Link cut to the chase. "Did he say anything to you about being asked to kill somebody?"

"Yeah! It all happened after we found that hit and run car, and then this guy is telling me somebody asked him to 'run somebody down.' He thought the guy was trying to kill *him*. I told Hicks."

"Oh dear Lord." Link didn't even try to hide the distain in his voice. "What did you tell Hicks?"

"Just that," Bryce replied. "We'd had a recent hit and run that seemed deliberate, and this guy talked about being asked to run someone down. Hicks blew me off. Told me my job was just to find people and leave police work to the detectives."

"Aw geez, I'm sorry you got treated like that. Just go around Hicks the next time. Listen, can you come down tomorrow and fill out a witness statement? We need to get that on the record."

"Sure," Bryce said, with a touch of fear in his voice. "Is Hicks going to know?"

"Oh, he's going to know," Link replied. "When I tell this to Wright, Hicks is going to know in a big way. Speaking for myself, and probably for Bob, you won't have to worry about Hicks again."

Chapter Fifteen
Ka-Boom

The glow was visible from blocks away. Against the dark, pre-dawn sky, the black billows of smoke were hard to pick out. But the flashing lights of multiple fire engines, police cars and ambulances created a reddish-blue hue that was unmistakable.

For a few minutes, as he crawled through backed-up traffic, Reeves was in denial. It had to be another house, any other house, than the one to which he was headed. The fire trucks and police tape would be an impediment to meeting up with Bonnie Shelton, but he'd get close enough that she could walk out, and hop in his vehicle. He'd already bought her a latte, so they could sneak directly to his office without stopping anywhere.

But as he got to the yellow tape, to the police officer directing traffic, Reeves realized he'd been deluding himself. He could see debris scattered in all directions from where Shelton's house had been. The rotten egg odor of natural gas still hung in the air.

"Officer, I know the woman who lives in that house. Is she okay?" Reeves asked. The response was brusque.

"Please keep it moving, sir. We've got traffic backed up a mile here. If you wanna find out what happened, check the news."

Reeves considered arguing, or parking and walking back to the scene. Maybe he could help. But then—no. He decided to follow the officer's orders and keep moving. *Really* moving.

* * *

"It's too hot for you to search the debris right now," the fire chief told Bryce. "If she's in there, she's gone anyway."

The scene was indeed not survivable, and flames were still flickering from pieces of the rubble that remained in place. Other portions of the rubble were scattered for blocks. One piece of plywood sheeting was 70 feet up in an evergreen tree. Firefighters had already named it the "mother slab," in deference to a huge piece of the Murrah Federal Building that hung precariously over rescuers at the 1995 Oklahoma City bombing.

The fire chief continued. "What I'd like you to do is check the brush and the greenbelt over there, for anyone who might have been tossed that way. If she fled out the back door just before it blew, she could have been thrown God-knows how far."

Bryce was okay with that. He'd worked Sierra on rubble during the Fragaria mudslide, and knew she could perform. But he never liked doing it. He knew that if firefighters couldn't locate the victim by themselves, he and Sierra would eventually be in the rubble, trying to pinpoint a place for them to dig. But for now, they'd do the work they were trained for, in a safer part of the scene.

Sierra was more than ready. Bryce had already put on her GPS collar and vest. The collar was really only for documentation, not tracking her. In this type of search, Sierra would not be out of his sight. He recorded her track only to prove exactly where his dog's nose had been.

"Okay, girl, let's go find!" Bryce said, in the brightest voice possible. They'd make a wide sweep off the street, right up to the neighboring house. Then they'd move into the greenbelt, circling around to the house on the other side.

Sierra always seemed to know when they weren't in the wilderness, and Bryce didn't have to remind her to stay close. She worked the neighbor's yard without so much as a twitch of her tail, and they moved into the greenbelt.

Bryce could immediately see that a lot of debris had blown there. The fire chief had been right, he thought, if someone was outside they easily could have been blown in that direction.

Sierra ignored most of what lay around, but suddenly began moving with purpose. Bryce picked up on the change of behavior and followed quickly but kept silent. Sierra began to jump over large bushes and push through wild hedges, a clue that she clearly had something. Dogs are like people—they're inherently lazy. When they suddenly start busting through thick brush, there's a reason. Bryce was hopeful they'd find someone, maybe even someone still alive.

"Dog 44, command," came the radio call.

"Dog 44, go ahead."

"Dog 44, command, you can secure from your assignment. We've located what we're looking for."

Bryce knew they'd found remains, and he'd been briefed to expect only one set in this residence. The woman lived alone, and none of her neighbors had ever known her to entertain an overnight guest.

"Dog 44, received. We'll be returning shortly."

But when Bryce refocused on Sierra, she was continuing to beat up a small area a few feet ahead. Bryce could hear her snorting and knew she was onto something, he just didn't know what.

"It's okay girl, we can go on back to the truck," was the command. Sierra ignored it and continued making smaller and smaller circles through the brush. "C'mon, Sierra, we gotta go." But Sierra continued to work.

Bryce decided to trust that Sierra had something worth seeing, and was rewarded when she sat with her nose pointed directly into a bush. Something there was giving off cadaver scent. Could it be a body part? Just because firefighters had found most of a body didn't mean a severed hand or toe couldn't have been propelled from the wreckage.

When Bryce got into the small clearing where Sierra sat, he could see quite a bit of debris from the house. Most of it looked like bathroom items. There was a bottle of mouthwash, completely intact. Next to it was a hairbrush, and Sierra's nose was radar-locked onto a bar of soap.

That initially confused Bryce, as Sierra had never had any penchant for perfumed items. Despite their strong smell, it wasn't human odor so Sierra had always ignored such things. However, after a few seconds of thought, Bryce realized what was happening. A bar of soap would have plenty of human scent. Sierra's nose could pierce through the overwhelming perfume odor to pick out the many human cells that would have been deposited when the bar was rubbed on every single part of the owner's body.

"Good girl!" Bryce said, deciding to reward the alert. "You da best you da best," and he tossed her ball a few feet away, into some neighboring brush. Sierra dashed to retrieve it, but as was her way, she laid down and began to mouth the ball. Bryce would have his usual difficult time getting it back from her.

Walking over to where Sierra lay with the ball, Bryce realized an entirely different part of the home had landed there. All the pieces of the bathroom had gone to the first spot, where Sierra found the soap. This new area was where most of the living room had landed. Bryce first spotted the TV remote, then a slipper. And then a notepad that seemed to have frisbee'd from the home. He could see writing on the pad.

All of the items in the clearing were slightly singed, but the blast wave had blown them clear of the house before fire took over. All were in remarkably good shape, including the notepad. Bryce couldn't imagine why it hadn't been shredded, or at least the individual pages ripped from the binding and scattered like confetti.

He continued staring at the notepad. How could something so delicate survive? But when he saw the writing, something in his brain suddenly jumped. Down the side of the first page was a list of numbers. Beside two of the numbers were names. He recognized one of them: Jason Manley.

"Where do I know that name from?" he asked himself. He'd heard it somewhere, remembering Katie was somehow involved. A friend of hers, perhaps?

And then, it hit him. "Holy crap! That's the dude Katie and Magnum found at the bottom of the cliff! Why would his name be on some list this lady kept?"

He mind ran through a list of what to do next and, more importantly, what not to do. He'd almost been kicked out of SAR on the Chimera case for scooping up bloody dirt that, at the time, nobody thought was evidence. But he'd also nearly missed grabbing the gloves at the homeless camp because Waylon Hicks was a jerk. To take or not to take. That was the question.

Then, he remembered Bob Wright's admonition to call any time something wasn't right. He didn't want to play that card recklessly, but figured he had a good enough batting average to risk a whiff. His call was answered on the second ring.

"Hey Bryce," was Wright's cheerful version of hello. With caller ID, he could always tell who was calling and tried to answer in a personal way. "I figured you'd be out at that thar blow'd up house."

"I am," Bryce said. "And you should be, too."

"Okaaay...whatcha got?"

"In some of the rubble, blown out into the woods, I found a notepad with a couple of names on it. One you'll remember: Jason Manley."

"I meet sooo many dead people," Wright joked. "Is he the guy off the bridge?"

"Nope, the one Katie found at the bottom of a cliff."

"Oh, right, over on Green Mountain. So who lived in the house that would have Manley's name on a sheet of paper?" was Wright's next question. "Maybe she was a friend or grieving relative."

"I'm told she was a retired older lady who lived alone," Bryce explained. "The fire chief told me all her relatives live out of state. Here's the interesting part. The name is on a list of numbers. Only two of the numbers have names with them, and I don't recognize the other one."

Bryce's radio crackled at that moment.

"Dog 44, command. Are you on your way back? I think I can see you out there."

Bryce delayed answering the radio and went back to his phone. "Bob…jeez. The fire chief is calling me back. He's called twice now but I don't want to leave this evidence."

"DON'T," was Wright's quick reply. "You're to stay there and keep eyes on that piece of paper. Don't touch it unless it's blowing away, and for damned sure don't let some firefighter traipse over it with their boots."

"Got it," Bryce said. "But what do I say to the fire chief? I don't want to say anything about this over the radio."

"It's okay if he's mad for a little while. I'm on the way and will square it when I get there. Or wait…let's do this. Tell him to come up on Tac 4 and contact me there."

"Wilco, stand by" was Bryce's response.

"Command, Dog 44."

"Dog 44, command. Go ahead."

"I need to stay right where I am until County 128 gets on-scene. He's available on Tac 4 if you need an explanation."

The fire chief had been around long enough to know he couldn't control every single detail. He also knew Bob Wright and was comfortable yielding to him, for a while at least. He definitely didn't want any disagreement aired over the radio.

"Okay, 44. Gotcha. I'll wait until 128 is here and get my explanation in person. He turned back to the rubble pile. "Hey

Dave," the chief said. "I need you to back out and not touch anything else."

The arson investigator took immediate offense. It was his stuff to touch.

"What's up? I'd like to get started..." was his response. The Chief cut him off.

"Something's up with this explosion. I don't know what, but Bob Wright from the Sheriff's Office is on the way over here and that dog handler has to stay right where he is. I assume the kid found something that interests Wright."

The investigator wanted to investigate. "I'll go over and see what the kid's got."

"I wish you wouldn't," the chief said. He had a way of asking that left no doubt he was telling. "Wright will be here soon enough, and if this becomes a joint investigation then so be it. Frankly, if it's a homicide it'll be good experience for you. You've done all kinds of fire and arson investigations, but you've never worked a straight-up murder. There's nobody better than Bob Wright to help you through the first one."

The flattery worked. The arson investigator suddenly saw the event as a way of building his resume, and backed down. But when Wright pulled up, the investigator was peppering him with questions before his car door was even shut.

Chapter Sixteen
Roundtable

Bryce had been to the Sheriff's inner office many times. Sometimes it had been for a "thank you," and once or twice when Bryce was in trouble for having overstepped. But this time was different. All he knew was that he'd been invited to something called a "roundtable discussion."

It wasn't just Bryce and the Sheriff. Undersheriff Bill Burns was sitting to the Sheriff's immediate right. Around the table were Bob Wright, Lenora Hogan, Jason Link and a distinguished looking man that Bryce hadn't met. The man introduced himself as Dr. Pete Jamieson, a pathologist from the coroner's office.

The Sheriff spoke first. "Bryce and Pete, this is new to you, but we're casting a wide net trying to figure out what's going on with all these deaths. We get everybody who's even touched the case in a room, and roundtable every piece of information we have. What doesn't click for one person will sound major bells for another. Bryce...Doctor J, I do have to tell you both that what's said in this room stays in this room. Understand?"

Bryce and Jamieson both quickly answered in the affirmative and the Sheriff continued.

"One person who's not here is Waylon Hicks. As most of you know, he's back in Patrol. I considered inviting him but decided he might be a bit divisive, so I'll just leave it at that. If we think of anything he might be able to contribute we'll have Bob follow up later, one-on-one. Okay, shall we get going?"

Everyone nodded. The Sheriff asked Wright to brief the room on where things stood.

"We've had about a dozen unusual deaths around the county over the past three months, each of which individually would mean nothing," Wright explained. "They all seem explainable, with the exception of Lenora's hit and run and a homeless guy stabbed to death. But the spike in deaths is what's concerning. Either something's going on, or the people of Kitsap County have gotten exceptionally clumsy all at the same time."

Jamieson jumped in. "Dex asked me to convey his concern, which I share," he explained, "We've both been around awhile and we've never seen anything like this. We're completely out of 'room at the inn' for any more dead bodies, especially ones that don't have families. That said, fishing expeditions always bother us. We weren't wild to hear you were looking into hospital deaths that were physician-attended."

"Everything we do is a balance," Sheriff Patterson responded. "We're used to it but it's probably new to you. Every time we stop a simple traffic violator we're balancing the need to protect their rights while making sure they don't have drugs, guns or bodies in their car. It's second nature for us, and I apologize if we got too casual with you."

"We'll get over it," Jamieson responded, "so long as we don't all end up in some federal penitentiary. Privacy laws are pretty strict."

Bryce watched the back-and-forth and wondered what he could possibly contribute. He was just a guy with a dog, who found bodies and occasionally evidence. Finding himself in a room full of high-powered investigators, Bryce was starting to wish Hicks was right—that he was just there to find the bodies.

The Sheriff brought the meeting back on topic, and Wright continued.

"We consider the hit-and-run to be case zero on our timeline," Wright said. "There might be other deaths before that, but it's the one that really brought this up on our radar. Lenora, how's that case going?"

"Nothing new, really. I still owe Bryce and Sierra their kisses for finding the vehicle. It might have eventually been called in as abandoned, but we don't send deputies on those anymore. Would our code-enforcement folks have recognized this was a suspect vehicle? No offense to them, but I doubt it. We simply wouldn't have this car if not for Bryce and Sierra."

Bryce blushed and looked down at the table, as Hogan continued. "This is as cold a car as I've ever seen. Somehow the current owner, who is presumably our hit-and-run suspect, assembled this car from three insurance total wrecks. Just finding three of the same model of car, wrecked and in tow yards, was a feat. Then he bought them from the insurance companies and reassembled them into one functioning SUV."

"State Patrol inspection?" the undersheriff asked.

"Yes, sir," Hogan replied. "He had all the right paperwork. The trooper inspected and saw that there were VINs from different vehicles, but the guy was totally honest that he was rebuilding wrecks. It's legal and lots of people do it. There was nothing to sound a warning bell for the trooper."

"Any video from the inspection?" was Link's question.

Hogan had that answer too. "I asked. The guy took the car to a VIN inspection station in Colville which is basically a metal shed. The Patrol had no video set-up there."

The Sheriff chimed in next. "Didn't you say earlier the registered address was in the middle of Wildcat Lake? How did DOL mail him his registration?"

Hogan had covered that base too. "Looks like he took the paperwork directly from the inspection to an equally tiny licensing office just down the road. They print paperwork on the spot, no mailing. And…you guessed it…no video cameras in that office. That's just kinda how things are in Colville."

The Sheriff sat back in his chair. "Wow, this guy's good. Sorta goes back to that old saying 'We only catch the dumb ones.' So what about the other cases?"

Wright spoke up. "The only other confirmed homicide is Hartman, the homeless guy. And it's a weird one. It looks like another guy's sword was used to kill our victim, but we've pretty much cleared the owner of the sword."

"How do you know that?" the undersheriff asked.

"Bryce, you've been pretty quiet here today. Why don't you explain, it was your discovery that cleared the guy."

"Um, okay sir. Thank you," Bryce was nervous speaking to the group. "Well, Sierra alerted on the cane but the blood didn't smear when he put it back which means it was dry which means it probably..."

Burns, the undersheriff, interrupted. "I'm sorry Bryce, there's something I'm not getting. I thought we were talking about a sword, and now you're talking about a cane."

"It was a sword that fit into a cane," Bryce explained. "There was blood on the blade...the sword part...that didn't smear when the killer put it back in the cane part. So it must have been dried before he did."

"And that matters how?" Burns asked. Bryce looked at Wright, who nodded as if to say "go ahead."

"Well, sir, the original suspect, the neighboring homeless guy, really does need a cane to walk. If he'd gone over and stabbed the guy he'd have had to put the blade back in the sheath pretty quickly to hobble away. But since the blood didn't smear, it must have been dry before the cane was reassembled."

"So that's it?" the undersheriff looked at Wright. "You cleared the guy because some blood *didn't* smear?"

"No, sir. We arrested him anyway and held him for a few days. What cleared him was that Bryce and Sierra found some gloves that were worn by the probable killer. The killer cut his hand during the killing and ditched them, probably while trying to put on a bandage."

"Ah, I remember the gloves now," Burns said. "One of the many nails in the career of Detective Hicks."

The Sheriff turned to Deputy Link. "You can't talk about that. It's a personnel matter. But yes, Hicks blew off collecting the gloves and it was only through Bryce's persistence that we got them at all. There was actually a laundry list of reasons I demoted him."

Hogan had been unfamiliar with that case, and asked the next obvious question. "So, any luck with DNA on the gloves?"

"No matches," Wright said. "The profile is now flagged, so if the DNA comes up in some other crime we'll get notified."

"Is there a reason the gloves didn't come to me?" Jamieson asked. "I'll send them to the lab in due time but things like that are part of the death scene."

"No sir, they're not something we'd ever send to you," Wright replied. "You get the body, and any clothing ON the body. Everything else is ours."

"We'll talk more about that later, detective," Jamieson pressed. "Let's not hold up the meeting with this detail."

The Sheriff moved on to the next case. "Now, what about the guy in the river?"

Wright handled that question, too. "Can't rule out suicide but there was no reason for it. I've done a ton of these where the family was in denial about someone's mental health issues, but this family didn't fit the pattern. No history of previous attempts and no reason for any stress in his life. The thing that really bothers me is the paint transfer."

"Paint transfer, like when cars collide?" the Sheriff asked.

"Exactly," Wright said. "There was paint from the bridge rail on the guy's cell phone case. But he wore it in the small of his back, which means he went over the rail backwards. Nobody jumps that way."

"That's it?" the undersheriff asked. "A little paint transfer is the only thing that makes you think he was pushed?"

"Well, that and the fact that there is absolutely no reason for this guy to commit suicide," Wright answered firmly. "I'll admit it's not much, but there's not much to any of this. The best we have is our gut feeling that something's wrong, and we can't find any common denominator. Right now, somebody who had no reason to commit suicide going over the rail backwards is as good as it gets."

Hogan came to her boss's defense. "Sir, I'm with Bob, and apparently the coroner's office. I've never seen a series of deaths like this, other than the Chimera Killer, and those were all obviously homicides right out of the gate. The fact that we have no evidence is starting to BE evidence."

"Okay, I get it," Burns backed off. "But when we go to prosecute these, we'll need to prosecute all of them or none of them. The evidence will be really thin in any one case, and if the others aren't charged, the prosecutor won't be able to talk about them."

"Let's not get ahead of ourselves, Bill," the Sheriff said. "Anything else on the bridge case?" he asked. Hearing nothing, he moved on to the best clue they had. "Tell me about this list that Bryce found."

Wright jumped in. "More nice work by our youngest member. Bryce, why don't you tell him what happened?"

"What happened isn't that important, sir," Bryce said, looking down at the table. "We found a list of numbers and names, and I recognized one of them."

Wright wasn't having any of Bryce's modesty. He turned away from Bryce and to face the rest of the group. "First his dog found a bar of soap. Think about it. What's on soap? Dead human skin cells. Sierra's just freaking awesome to get through the fragrance on the soap to smell the dead human. Then, a couple of shrubs away, Bryce sees a piece of paper and recognizes a damned name." He turned to Bryce. "This is why you're here today, young man, and don't play all 'aw shucks' with us."

Bryce's face turned red, and he admitted the obvious. "Okay, we found a really *helpful* piece of paper. But it's what you all do with it that matters. We just find stuff."

"We're grateful, Bryce," The Sheriff said. "You've done more than we could have asked. But you're right, we need to figure out what the paper means."

"I worked that case personally, sir," Wright said. "The victim was retired and living alone, but she had previously worked for an insurance brokerage. We think the numbers were a list of policy numbers."

"Wait a minute," Burns said. "I thought we'd already eliminated insurance as a motive."

Wright kept his cool. "Hicks did, if you recall the spreadsheet. But all we really knew was that the families weren't beneficiaries. A couple of the widows are for-real losing their homes. But a list of numbers with the name of at least one potential murder victim changes the game."

Burns again. "What about the other name?"

Wright had to refer to his notes. "Taylor…Jason Taylor. No real info on him, not sure why he'd be on the list."

"I am," Hogan said, the fury visible in her face. "That's the guy the E-R doc thought might have been killed by his wife. Hicks came back from the autopsy swearing up and down it was a rock-solid natural death. It was supposedly something un-fake-able with his aorta."

"I did that autopsy," Jamieson interjected. "It was un-fake-able."

"Then why is his name on a list of murder victims?" Hogan asked.

"We don't know that these are all murder victims," Jamieson replied. "I'll grant you we've had a spike in deaths, but until we know for sure we have to take them at face value."

"If it turns out Taylor wasn't murdered, then our whole theory goes down the drain," Hogan lobbed back, "and that's in direct conflict with every one of my instincts."

"Let's just go with what we have," Undersheriff Burns interjected, trying to calm the water. He looked over at Wright. "What are you doing to figure out what these numbers mean?" he asked.

"If they're policy numbers sir, we first need to figure out what insurance company," Wright said. "Then we need to see if the policy numbers listed all have death claims."

Burns took his questions in another direction. "Are we sure the explosion that killed the Shelton woman was an accident?"

"No, we're not," Wright said. "The explosion tore things up so bad the arson folks can't determine a cause. It's the same old absence of evidence thing."

"Bob and Lenora, your next task is to figure out if those numbers are indeed policy numbers, from what insurance company, and if any of our other victims had similar…wait a minute." He paused, thought, and started again. "Didn't I hear Hicks say all the insurance companies talk to one another? If they'd paid a bunch of sketchy claims in the same community they'd have noticed."

Wright responded with a clarification. "You're right sir. Along with the widows not getting any money, we did check with the insurance association. They keep a database of large claims, and none of these folks were on it. But I don't completely trust large corporations—I think we need to run this down ourselves."

Burns jumped in again. "What about the firm she used to work for? Would they recognize the numbers?"

"Probably," Wright said. "We tried making contact, but the office was closed. We'll go back in a day or two and see what the owner has to say. The owner's name is Alan Reeves."

"A former employee gets blown to bits and the office is just closed on a weekday?" Burns again, drilling down. "I mean, she was retired. It's not like they're so traumatized they can't work."

Wright tried to keep his exasperation from showing. "Sir, I don't know why the office was closed, and if it stays closed then maybe we've got something. It's on my list to follow up, and I'll let you know if things turn hinky."

Patterson sensed it was time to end the meeting. "If the list Bryce found is a list of victims, but we have somebody on it who's clearly NOT a victim, that screws up our whole theory. The big take away from this is to find Mr....what was it...Reeves?...and see what he knows about this list."

"You got it boss," Wright said. "Lenora, you and I will double team Reeves so we can't possibly miss a call-back."

The Sheriff spoke again. "I'd like to go back over one case...the guy in the water." He turned in his chair. "Bryce, we need to talk."

"If you mean me going in the water sir, I understand that was a mistake." Bryce now hung his head for real.

"Going in the water is not a big deal, but slipping out of your life vest is what got my attention…"

"I know, sir," Bryce interrupted. His nervousness was taking over. "Bob…Detective Wright explained about trading rescuers for victims, and the time he wrecked his car. I got all that. It won't happen again."

The rest of the room sat in stunned silence. It was unheard of for this Sheriff, with his style of leadership, to correct a subordinate in front of others. He'd never done that.

"I'm glad you do, because I want you on my team for a long time," the Sheriff said. "But I also don't want to dwell on the negative." He picked up his phone. "Karen, would you have Firefighter Tarana join us please?"

Bill Tarana had been asked to show up a half-hour AFTER the meeting started, and had patiently waited as those in the roundtable had hashed through all their cases-that-might-not-be-cases.

"Thanks for waiting, Bill," the Sheriff said, extending a hand. "I'm Elroy Patterson and I'm glad you're okay."

"Good to meet you, Sheriff, and I'd have waited all day if you'd asked," Tarana said, turning to Bryce. "Is this the young man who took off his life vest for me?"

"We've discussed that," the Sheriff said. "Bryce has gotten the message."

"Well, he's going to get it one more time from me," Tarana said, his eyes starting to well up. "I'm eternally grateful that you did what you did, but you shouldn't have done it. You should not be trading your young life for an old goat like me. I'm not worth it."

Tarana walked around the table and put his hands on Bryce's shoulders. Bryce stood up, and the two hugged like only rescued and rescuer can. The eyes of everyone else in the room sprung leaks at that moment.

"Sir, I'm glad you're okay," Bryce managed to choke out. "I get that it was risky, and none of you will get close to giving me the grief I got from Katie—she's my girlfriend. But in the end it all worked out okay and that's good enough for me."

The Sheriff reached in his breast pocket and took out something shiny that Bryce had never seen before. The object was round, and a little bigger than a silver dollar. "Ever heard of a Sheriff's coin, young man?" Patterson asked.

"No, sir."

The coin was two-sided, with a small replica of the Sheriff's Office badge on one side. On the other was a rendering of the memorial stone outside the building inscribed with the names of fallen deputies.

"The tradition of coins started in the military, with what were called 'challenge coins,'" the Sheriff explained. "It was a drinking game. If you didn't have your unit's challenge coin you had to buy a round for your buddies."

"I'm not old enough to drink," Bryce answered.

"And this is not a challenge coin. It's a Sheriff's coin and that's different. There's no drinking involved. We don't give these out to memorabilia collectors, either. This only goes to people who've done some service to the Sheriff's office. I had them made up so I can reward first-rate behavior on the spot. Now despite some occasional back-and-forth, I consider the fire department part of the Sheriff's family. You did them a great service, which means you did me a great service. Now hold out your hand like we're going to shake."

Bryce did as he was told.

"The history of coins is that they were given almost surreptitiously, by sergeants to their young soldiers. They were slipped from one to the other during a handshake." And with a firm handshake, the Sheriff slipped Bryce his first Sheriff's coin.

Wright looked back at Bryce, expecting his would be the happiest face in the room. But instead of looking at his coin, Bryce just looked puzzled. "What's up, bud?" Wright asked. "You okay?"

"Ahh, I'm just seeing boogie men," Bryce replied. "No biggie. Sheriff, thanks for the coin."

The Sheriff excused everyone from the meeting, but Bryce departed with that nagging feeling he'd felt once before. Despite Wright's previous admonition, he just couldn't bring himself to say it out loud.

Chapter Seventeen
Big Fish, Small Pond

Of all the things that Bryce and Katie had in common, most related to dogs. But they also shared a distinct hate for stuffy dinner parties. It was one thing to have a bunch of friends over for pizza and games. But sitting down at a dinner table and listening to adults talk about work stress or medical procedures was the worst.

Katie was sitting to Bryce's right, across from the most obnoxious man on the planet. Ken Feideke was some kind of business executive, and a legend in his own mind. At the moment, he was on a tear, bragging about his expense account. He'd taken clients to every kind of restaurant, golf course, amusement park and race track one could imagine. He even looked at Bryce's dad, winked, and said "why don't you join us the next time we go to Thailand, Brian? They've got some really interesting *shows* over there, if you know what I mean."

"I do know what you mean, Ken," was the elder Finn's patient response. "I was in the Air Force and did time at Ubon Royal. We'd go into town, but those *shows* really didn't interest me."

Fiedeke tried adjusting his approach. "They have great golf, too. Labor's so cheap I swear...they can hire somebody to individually clip each blade of grass on the green."

"But how would you justify taking me?" Bryce's Dad asked. "I already have one of your policies, just to cover my funeral expenses. So it's not like you're trying to wheel and deal me into a major purchase."

"You're on the client list and that's all that matters, my friend," Fiedeke said. "All corporate is interested in is marketing, marketing and marketing. I get my chops busted if I'm *not* taking people to dinner or golf. It's how we build our business."

"And tell me again about your company?" Brian Finn asked. "I know it's life insurance, and it WAS really cheap. But how does this work?"

"A better mousetrap for the insurance world," the tipsy executive answered. "We invented something called high-volume, low-premium life insurance. It's all automated, and easy to get. Low premiums, a minimum of medical hassles and the only catch is that we don't pay much. Our biggest policy pays only fifty grand if you croak. Yours is what, 15 thou? Like you said, enough for a funeral."

"Who else do you sell to?" was Brian Finn's obvious next question.

"Lotsa businesses who want to offer some kind of insurance plan for their employees but can't afford to play with the big boys," Fiedeke said. "And lemme tell ya, small business people really respond to being wined and dined. You take some guy who has four employees and host him at a golf tournament...the man is yours."

Brian Finn's face reflected his skepticism. "That pays off?"

"Big time," Fiedeke said, finishing his fourth glass of wine. "These small businesses are all hiring young kids…millennials. They're healthy as horses and they move between jobs quickly. So we collect premiums for a few months, maybe a year, and the kid moves on. The employer cancels the policy and we're off the hook. Every bit of premium we collected for that year is now pure profit and we'll never have to pay a claim."

Bryce's father was intrigued. "So what's the connection to Thailand? Do you just like the place?"

"No, that's where we farmed out all of our I-T and corporate services," Fiedeke bragged. "It's an emerging market for them, so we take people to visit our 'central office.' Thailand is actually cheaper than India, if that's possible."

"Well, that's always a plus," replied Bryce's dad, grasping for something to praise. "So this works? You've actually figured out how to write insurance policies for people who aren't gonna die?"

Fiedeke wrinkled his nose. "The last few months have kinda sucked. We've had a few more deaths than our number-crunchers would have expected, but it seems like just a normal swing. A few more for a period, and then a dry spell hopefully."

Bryce's ears perked up at the prospect of a spike in deaths, and a dry spell. That was exactly what the Sheriff's Office had experienced, so maybe it did happen. He decided to listen for a bit and let his parents' guest keep bragging.

"The best part," Fiedeke said, "is that by the standards of most insurance companies we're an incredibly small outfit. The big boys don't see us as competition, and the regulators figure we're too small to worry about. So we're making money hand over fist, and we're completely under everybody's radar."

The magic words. Under the radar. Bryce was now totally engrossed in their previously boring guest's commentary. Watching the man start his fifth glass of wine, Bryce decided it was time to step in, gingerly.

"How many people do you have to insure to pay for one that dies?" Bryce asked.

"Well, it's not that simple, little buddy," Fiedeke said. "We invest the premiums we get so there's income on that. We make money on your money between the time you pay us and the time you die. If you don't die, we just keep making money on your money."

"So when somebody dies, you look into it?" Bryce asked. "Reports, documentation, proof that they're really dead?"

"Nahh, the Thais handle that," was the condescending answer. "It's all about numbers and paperwork. They get a scanned copy of a death certificate and they check a box on their screen. The computer does a wire transfer to whoever was named as the beneficiary."

"So, what if somebody sent you a fake death certificate?" was Bryce's next question.

"Dunno. I just sell the insurance and collect the money. I'm curious about why you're curious. Thinking of a career in insurance?"

"Not at all," Bryce said. There was no way he'd offer up the real reason for his interest. "I'm not good enough at numbers. If you had a cluster of deaths, would your computer tell you?"

In what was a first for their relationship, Katie gave Bryce a slight kick under the table, and a look that clearly said "you're not supposed talk about SAR cases."

"What, you mean all in one place?" Fiedeke asked. "I doubt it. The Thais certainly don't know what's where in the US. And we don't participate in the database."

"What database?" Bryce asked.

"The National Life Insurance Database...we call it the 'bucket list,' as it's everybody who's kicked the bucket. The big boys all got together back in the '60s and decided to share information on policies and claims. They wanted to make sure somebody wasn't buying big policies for their spouse or business partner and then killing them."

"Seems like a good idea," Bryce opined. "Why aren't you part of that?"

"Can't be, and don't wanna be," was the answer. "They put a lower limit of $50,000 on policies in order for companies to participate. And like I said, our goal is to stay under the radar. If we start playing with those guys, they'll start selling their insurance cheaper and put us out of business. We like it that none of them know what we do. We don't go to their conferences, we don't play in their charity golf tournaments, and we don't send them fruitcakes at Christmas."

"And you don't tell their database when one of your customers dies," Bryce shot back. Katie kicked him again.

"We call them clients, or insureds," Fiedeke said. "But yeah, we don't see a need to tell anybody our business."

"That's very interesting, sir," Bryce said, finally taking Katie's hints. "Thanks for filling me in."

Bryce had waited a respectable amount of time before excusing himself from the table. Katie joined him, and they were soon in his dad's home office, going through drawers.

"Should we be doing this?" Katie asked. "Does your dad know...?"

"He already showed me their wills and where they keep their policies, so he's not going to care that we're looking at them now," Bryce replied. "I just wanna see the policy dad has with Mr. Fiedeke."

Katie was puzzled. "Why look at it? Your dad's not dead."

"It's the policy numbers," Bryce explained. "Remember, Sierra found that list and we wondered what the numbers meant. Here it is..."

Bryce looked at the paperwork and whistled. "It's exactly the same combination of letters and numbers. And the number's in a box labelled 'policy numbers.' The list is exactly what we thought it was."

"But why couldn't Wright or Hicks or somebody trace it back to the company?" Katie asked, and then answered her own question. "Oh my God, they're not in the database. They're 'under the radar.' His whole business model."

"Which not only explains why Hicks couldn't find them," Bryce said, "but it's probably why the killer picked that company in the first place. He knew it would all be under the radar. We gotta call Wright.

Bryce hit the speed dial on his phone, and was answered on the second ring.

"Hey Bryce, how you doin' buddy?" was Wright's usual greeting. Bryce was nervous, and didn't respond to the question.

"Hey, Bob. Am I...interrupting anything?" Bryce asked.

"You're never an interruption, and every time you call me something interesting develops." Bob Wright had had his own glass or two of wine. "You're a crap-magnet, you know."

Bryce's forehead furrowed. "I'm sorry, a what-magnet?"

"A crap-magnet," Wright explained. "That's what we call cops who are always getting into crap. They're no different than the rest of us, except that crap seems to find them. They walk into a convenience to buy a bag of chips and they end up in the middle of a robbery and shootout. Y'know...crap."

"Well, I have to agree that more than my share of crap has come my way," Bryce said. "Katie too."

"Yup, you two are equal opportunity crap-magnets. You gonna get married when you're older?" Wright asked. It might have been three glasses of wine.

"Sure seems that way, doesn't it?" Bryce said, deliberately not looking at Katie.

"I can hear your phone," she hissed. "Seems that way?"

Bryce was by now completely flustered, trying to walk a line between a drunk detective and his girlfriend. "Look...um, there's a reason I called. Can we talk about insurance?"

"What, are you trying to buy some?" Wright asked.

"No, but we just met somebody who sells some. His goal is to stay under the radar, so to speak, and he might just be under yours."

Bob Wright was now completely sober.

* * *

"Well that'll be the last time I run my mouth at a dinner party," Fiedeke said. "I tell some kid how my business works and the next morning the cops are here."

"You're not in trouble, sir," Wright explained. Lenora Hogan sat next to him in the small conference room. "Bryce told us what you said about your business, and there's nothing illegal about it. I kinda wish I'd thought of it first. You're not a suspect in anything, and in fact, you might be a victim."

"How so?" Fiedeke asked, still a bit defiant.

"We found a list of numbers, with a couple of names, at the scene of a death. Bryce looked at his dad's policy, and it looks like the numbers we have are pretty similar to the way you issue policy numbers. Would you be willing to look at the list?"

"I suppose," Fiedeke replied. "You think my policyholders were murdered?"

"If the numbers line up, then yes," Hogan interjected. "We've had an inordinate number of accidental deaths. Individually there'd be no cause for alarm. But taken together it's too many to all be coincidental."

Fiedeke almost looked relieved, leaned into the table, and lowered his voice. "That would actually be great freaking news, at least for my company. We had this run of crazy death claims. They killed our past two quarters of profit. I couldn't say it at the table last night, but we were starting to question our business model. If it turns out these were murders, then our business is still viable."

"Well, I hope this works out for everybody," Hogan said. It was clear that Fiedeke was responding better to an attractive woman than to an older detective, and Wright had no issue stepping back.

Hogan pressed. "So would you be willing to look at our list and see if they're policy numbers first, and then if they're ones you've paid out on?"

"I think we'd better," was Fiedeke's quick response. "Show me your list."

Fiedeke got into his computer, and Hogan sidled up beside him to get a look. Just as Wright had no ego about stepping back, Hogan had no problem using her womanhood to gain the cooperation of a reluctant witness.

The logjam had been broken, and information started flooding in. The numbers were indeed policy numbers, and each had been the subject of a paid claim. Fiedeke was furious.

"Each one of these claims was bulletproof, but they were all from around here," he fumed. "We should have geofenced our system, so that if too many claims came up in one area we'd get notified."

"How much are you out?" Hogan asked.

"That's the good news," Fiedeke replied. "Since we only issue small policies, our total loss is probably under a million bucks."

"A million bucks is still a great motive for murder," Hogan replied. "So what are the common denominators with these policies? That's what'll lead us to whoever did this."

Fiedeke spent a few minutes looking over the policies. Each had been taken out by a different party, and each had a different beneficiary. "These policies are as normal as they come. If anything, they're too perfect. Look, every one of them has a death certificate signed off by your coroner's office...unless they're forgeries."

Hicks had been the one to review death certificates before being bounced back to patrol. But Hogan knew there were death certs for each case, and hadn't bothered looking at them.

"Here!" Fiedeke exclaimed. "That's it. These policies were all issued by the same agency. Somebody there had to know what was happening."

"The same agency?" Hogan asked.

"Right," Fiedeke replied. "We don't sell directly to the client, we work though an agent. We might schmooze an insured to get them interested, but we hook them up with an agent to write the deal."

"So at the very least, the agent would have been in on it?" Hogan parroted back for confirmation.

"Hell, I can't see anybody pulling this off except an agent. And if he had experience with life insurance, he'd certainly know the various ways people manage to kill themselves. This is too perfect. I wanna kill this guy myself."

"Well, let's not get carried away, and I'll forget you said that," Hogan said. "So who is this agent?"

"The agent of record is...Alan Reeves."

Chapter Eighteen
You're Who?

"Thanks for coming over, Dex," the Sheriff said. "I know it's short notice, but things are moving fast. I didn't want to risk missing something."

Dex Lawson was the elected coroner, who oddly enough took office the same year as Sheriff Patterson. The two had campaigned together and had become both professional allies and personal friends.

"No problem," Lawson replied. "My customers aren't going anywhere."

"I assume Dr. Jamieson filled you in about the last meeting?," the Sheriff asked.

"He did."

"Good. And you know everyone in the room?"

Other than Lawson, the room was made up of the same people who had attended the last roundtable. Undersheriff Burns, Lenora

Hogan and Bob Wright. Even Bryce had been invited back—although he wasn't sure why.

"Yes, I know everybody here," Good to see you, Bryce"

The Sheriff started the conversation. "It appears we finally have a decent development in this rash of deaths, and I want everyone's input. Bob, would you brief the room?"

"Yes sir," Wright responded. "Sometimes it's better to be lucky than good, but in this case we were both," he said. "The lucky part was Bryce's parents had a dinner party where some guy had too much wine and started running his mouth about a new way of doing life insurance. The good part was that Bryce was at that party—and was sharp enough to connect the dots."

"So this is an insurance scam?" Undersheriff Burns pressed.

"Looks like it. Bryce tipped us to this insurance exec. We found him, and it turns out he's from the company that insured all our victims. It was breaking their business model, but they didn't want to tell anybody for fear investors would pull out. Bryce, all of the numbers on that list you found were indeed life insurance policy numbers and as I said, all had death claims."

"So why didn't this come up before?" Burns asked.

"It was a business strategy," Wright said. "They'd found a way to sell insurance to people who were almost certainly NOT going to die, through their employers. Once the employee left the company there was zero chance of the insurance company ever having to pay. So every penny of premium they'd collected went in their pocket."

The light went on for Burns. "So they didn't report claims 'cuz they didn't want the other companies to pick up on their strategy."

"Exactly," Wright added. "If that company executive hadn't accidentally spilled the beans over at Bryce's house, we'd probably still be spinning our wheels."

"Well that's definitely both lucky and good," Burns mused. "So where are we now with the case?"

"The agent of record for the policies is one Alan Reeves. He's somewhere between a person-of-interest and a suspect," Wright said. "It's hard to believe all of these policies could have turned into death claims without him raising a concern."

"His record?" Hogan asked.

"Nothing," Wright said, shaking his head. "No criminal record, no license violations with the Insurance Commissioner, and his firm even has a triple-A rating from the Better Business Bureau."

Hogan was skeptical. "Very few people pick murder as their first crime. Maybe he's just clueless?"

"That's why we're not calling him a suspect...yet," Wright responded. "The downside is that he seems to have gone off radar after the explosion at Ms. Shelton's house. For those of you who aren't familiar with all the details, she had recently retired from the firm. When I checked Reeves' credit cards for activity, it all just stopped the day of the explosion."

"So he blows up the Shelton house and then blows town?" the Sheriff offered.

"Could be," Wright said. "Even at only 50 grand a pop there were enough payouts for him to live a lavish life in some country with a favorable exchange rate and no extradition treaty."

Burns turn. "So what are we doing to find him?"

Wright already had a plan. "I've got a couple of SWAT guys in plainclothes watching his house. If he shows up there we've certainly got probable cause to detain and ask some questions. The prosecutor is reviewing a search warrant for both his home and business, though it's not really clear where his business is. There are a couple of addresses listed with the Insurance Commissioner."

"And if he's not anywhere?" Burns queried.

"Then he gets elevated to 'suspect' and we get the US Marshals looking for him," Wright replied.

"Does he have any other links to any of the victims?" Hogan asked. "I mean, besides writing their insurance?"

"That's the next angle to figure out," Wright replied. "Right now I need you with us for the search warrants, but once that's done let's look for those links."

Wright's cell phone buzzed with a text. "Wow, that's a first," he said. "The deputy prosecutor has approved the search warrant in record time and with no edits. We need to haul over there right now so we can get it in front of a judge."

Wright and Hogan got up to leave, but the Sheriff cleared his throat first.

"I'd like to remind everyone that what's said in this room stays in this room," he said. "If Reeves blew up Ms. Shelton's house to keep us from finding the list of policies, God knows how far he'll go to hide what he's done. Bryce and Dex, could you hang back, please?"

"Sure," Bryce said.

"No problem," the coroner responded.

With Hogan and Wright gone, the Sheriff turned to Bryce. "I have a bad feeling about this one. Bryce, we almost got you, Katie and Sierra killed on the last big case. I don't want us getting anywhere near that kind of outcome again."

"Me neither, sir," Bryce said.

"I figured not," said the Sheriff. "Can you keep an eye on Katie? She doesn't need to know everything but just ask her to be careful. If either of you spot anybody following you, or anything suspicious around home, back out and call 9-1-1, okay?"

"Um, okay…" Bryce replied. "But I'm just a dog handler. I just look for evidence."

"Well, you're a dog handler who's given our killer reason to be mighty pissed at you," the Sheriff warned. "You found the car that kicked this off, you found the list of policy numbers, and you were smart enough to figure out that a rambling drunk had meaningful information. So far he's only killed for money, but revenge is a powerful motive."

"I'll be careful, sir," Bryce replied. "I'll let Katie know too, but she'll want the whole story."

"Can't give it to her at this point," the Sheriff reminded him. "Just let her know the two of you are involved in something and until we get this Reeves guy in custody we need you both on alert."

The coroner interrupted. "Sheriff, I'm sorry, but I gotta go."

"Okay, but the admonition applies to you, too," the Sheriff said. "Nobody outside this room knows where we're headed with the case."

"Gotcha," was the coroner's reply. "Now that we've got the full list of names off the policy list I'm going to review those autopsies to see if there's anything we missed."

* * *

Wright, search warrant in hand, was nearly at Reeves' home when his radio squawked. Hogan, right behind in her own Crown Vic, also heard the call.

"128 from 54, on Tac 1," came the call. Denny Neilson was a hard-as-nails SWAT operator. The only apparent humor in his life was his call sign, which he took from an old TV show.

"Car 54 where are you?" Wright called in return.

"54...I'm right where you sent me, sitting on Reeves' house. Looks like our boy just got home."

"128, that's great. Hogan and I have the warrant and are about five out. If he leaves, grab him but I'd sure like to catch him inside and unaware. Would love to see what's up on his computer screen, or which drawers he has open."

"54, understood."

After Wright and Hogan had continued for another few blocks, the radio came to life a second time.

"128 from 54...our guy just went out the back on foot. He's gone over a fence. 63 is in foot pursuit and I'm trying to get out ahead of them both with the car."

"128...over the back fence? Is that northbound? We're coming from that direction."

"54, yes. Keep coming and make some noise. We'd like to get him to go to ground."

Wright and Hogan turned on their sirens, and not because they needed to clear traffic. The hope was that the sound of approaching sirens would make their man feel trapped and cause him to hide. Once he was stationary, he'd be much easier to find either through eyeball searching or with a police K9.

Wright broke radio procedure. "Lenora, cut over to 56th. I'll go down 54th. That'll make it sound like the whole world is coming."

The two continued to approach the scene, as their man continued to hop fences and cut through backyards as he unknowingly headed straight for them. Neilson could hear the other sirens, but so far their subject was showing no signs of slowing down or looking for a place to hide.

"63, subject is armed," was the next radio call. Wright was amazed at how calm the SWAT operators could be when things were falling apart around them. The next call was just as calm.

"54, shots fired, subject down."

It took about another minute for Wright and Hogan to arrive, to find Neilson and his partner rendering first aid to the person who'd just fired on them. CPR doesn't really work on people who've been shot. It just tends to make them bleed out faster. But the two SWAT officers made a good effort, both for their own consciences and any nearby cameras.

"Everybody okay?" Wright asked. "I mean our people…anybody hit?"

"We're good," Neilson responded. "I'm the shooter."

Wright went into investigator mode, even though his co-worker had just nearly been killed. "Let's get aid here and get you relieved. Don't talk to anybody but me about the shooting, and you know what I'm going to ask."

Cops are employees just like anybody else and generally expected to tell the boss what they did during their workday. But when an officer is also facing criminal charges after a shooting, their Miranda rights kick in. The investigator is expected to walk a line between the two worlds, getting neither too much nor too little info.

"Let's get him out of the CPR loop," Wright said to Hogan, pointing at Neilson. "Glove up and keep it going until fire gets here. We'll let them decide it's time to stop."

Hogan understood what was expected and she leaned in to take a round of compressions, ever so gently nudging Neilson to the side. Wright put a hand on his shoulder and said, "Let's go, Denny. You've done all you can, we'll take it from here."

"I'm good, man," was the defiant response. "It was his choice."

"Don't talk to me about that now," Wright said. "That's the adrenaline talking and it's bad procedure. I have about six questions to ask you and then we're going to hook you up with some help."

"I don't need any help," Neilson continued. "I'm good with what happened and I'll talk to you right-damn-now."

"We're only going to do the public safety interview now," Wright said softly. "Then we're going to hook you up with peer support or a chaplain or whatever you want. This is still a shooting, even if you're an old hand SWAT guy."

Neilson took a few breaths and appeared to acquiesce.

"Okay…the six questions. Ask away," he said.

"You know the first two," Wright said. "What direction did you fire, and what direction did our suspect fire?"

"I had just hopped out of the car and my door wasn't even closed yet," Neilson offered. "I blocked his path. He fired north, right up the road there. I fired south, and I think all my shots were hits."

"Good," Wright said. "Do you think your shots could have injured anyone behind him, or his shots hit anyone behind you?"

"Nope. 63 and I might have had a crossfire situation, but he moved to the side. No innocent hits."

"Again good," Wright repeated. "The last two are evidence and witnesses. Point out either."

"My shell casings are right there by the car. There should be two…"

"Don't tell me how many times you fired," Wright admonished. "You're not expected to and everybody's always wrong. You were standing next to the car, right?"

"Right, so any shell casings that came out of my gun should be near the driver's door," Neilson explained. "Looks like our dead guy was using a revolver so no casings over there."

"Witnesses?" Wright asked.

"Just 63 so far as I know. He was in foot pursuit right behind. No telling if any of the neighbors were peeking out their windows."

"Okay, good job. You're done," Wright said. "I need your gun and will probably have your car towed. We'll get you a ride home and a spare gun from the off…"

At that moment, the unmistakable sound of a major explosion blew over them. Even blocks from the scene, the blast wave compressed their chests and made their ears hurt. They watched open-mouthed as a 4x8 sheet of plywood, shingles still attached, sailed over their heads like a Frisbee and landed in a nearby yard.

"Jesus, he booby trapped the house!" Neilson exclaimed.

"Had any of our guys gone in?" Wright asked.

"Hell, no," Neilson said. "63 and I were the only ones here. We were waiting for you with the search warrant."

The two men ran hell-bent-for-leather toward the sound of the explosion. Along the way, they saw other homes with windows blown out and mailboxes flattened. As they got closer, they saw entire homes shifted off their foundations. The only home that was completely gone was Reeves'.

Wright got on the radio. "128, Westcom. You're gonna get a bunch of calls about an explosion out here. I'm no fireman but I think this is a two, maybe a three-alarm response. And extra medical. We've got to search all the neighboring houses for victims."

"Westcom, 128. We've had calls and if it's a gas explosion it's automatically a third alarm."

"128 good. I still need one paramedic over at our original scene with the wounded suspect. Everybody else comes here to the house. And we'll need a bunch of our units for traffic and crowd control."

"Westcom, understood. The medic unit just arrived at your other scene, we'll get everybody else coming your way."

"128, thank you." Wright ignored the fact that Neilson wasn't supposed to be doing police work after a shooting. For the time being, he needed his help. The two men began checking neighboring houses for injured persons. They'd cleared the two closest to them just as the first fire engines arrived at the scene.

"These two are clear," Wright hollered to the battalion chief as he came down from the truck. "You'll want to start with the houses across the street and behind. I've got units coming for traffic control."

"We'll take it from here," the white-shirted firefighter offered. "All your guys okay?"

"We're fine," said Wright. "Do what you gotta do, Chief, but please keep in mind this is a crime scene. Do your best to protect the evidence unless you're saving a life."

"Not our first arson," the Chief replied, his nose slightly out of joint. "Bigger scene than most, but we know what we're doing."

Wright offered an apology. "Of course you do. Stuff's just getting weird here and it doesn't need to get any weirder. Didn't mean to offend."

"No offence taken," the Chief lied. He moved on to direct his own team to extinguish fires and check nearby buildings for dead or injured.

By the time Wright and Neilson got back to the scene of the shooting, paramedics had declared the man dead. He would remain covered by a blanket while investigators worked the scene, and only then would he be removed to the Coroner's office.

Wright had Neilson wait in Wright's car, as Neilson's was being towed. Wright had been on the phone arranging peer support and a chaplain when his radio squawked again.

"128 from 173," was the call. 173 was a rookie deputy, and had been assigned to do crowd control at the explosion. *"Can you come back to the SE corner of the explosion scene? I've got somebody you should talk to."*

"I'm a little busy right now," Wright answered. "Can you take a statement or something?"

"173 I really think you should talk to this person. He says it's his house that blew up."

That got Wright's attention. "What's his name?"

"Alan Reeves," was the reply.

Wright almost jumped from his car and hurried over to meet Mr. Reeves. As he did, he looked over at the blanketed body at the center of his own crime scene.

"Well, well, well, my dead friend," he thought. "If Alan Reeves is alive and outside his former house, who the hell are you?"

Chapter Nineteen

Dead Man Talking

Detective Sgt. Bob Wright didn't get confused much. But he was across the yellow tape from someone he thought had just been shot to death. His forehead was a bit wrinkled.

"If you're Alan Reeves," he asked, "who is the dead guy over there?"

"It's gotta be Dominic," Reeves replied. "Dominic Romero. I bought his business. He's dead?"

"He tried to shoot a cop," Wright said. "Annnd probably had something to do with this house blowing up. I take it this was your house, Mr. Reeves?"

"Yes it's my house, and he's not my friend. He killed Bonnie and...Jesus...he blew up both our houses," Reeves started to prattle from the stress. "I was just trying to sort out all the paperwork and it got Bonnie killed and now all this..."

Prattling was good. Reeves had been a suspect, and still was. But Wright didn't want to risk shutting him down with a Miranda warning. He decided to gently question Reeves as a witness right where he stood—a location he'd walked to of his own volition.

"I'm guessing the Bonnie you referenced is Bonnie Shelton. How do you know her?"

Reeves started to cry. "I convinced her to come out of retirement to help me figure out the office filing system. Dominic wouldn't help, even after all the money I paid him. Bonnie was the next best thing."

"I'm gonna need you to slow down. You bought a business from the fellow who's dead over there?" Wright asked.

"Well, I guess it's him. Who else would it be? I wanted to expand my brokerage...I'm in insurance. Dominic was retiring, so I bought his firm, intending to fold it into mine. Are you sure that's him?"

"We'll have you take a look once the scene's been processed," Wright allowed, "but what you're telling me actually makes sense. You hired Bonnie to help you sort out paperwork in your new business?"

"She knew the office inside and out," Reeves blurted between sobs. "I needed help but...God...I got her killed."

Wright decided to shut up and let the man continue uninterrupted. No point in using a bunch of hard-nosed, all-business cop-speak if a little patience would get all the same answers voluntarily.

"His record system was 'filing by piling,'" Reeves continued. "We had figured out most everything, but there were a few policies we couldn't track down. The couple we did work through had death claims, and that made us both very nervous."

"Okayyy…" Wright liked where this was going, but kept his mouth shut.

"We had a list of policy numbers we couldn't reconcile. Bonnie was going to come back for a second day and try to run things down. When I got to her house, the firefighters were there. I split."

Time for a zinger. Wright needed an explanation for behavior that looked really bad. "Yes, you did split, and you haven't been seen since."

"I figured if he killed her he'd try to kill me. And it looks like I was right," Reeves said.

"So where ya been?" Wright asked, getting closer to the Miranda line. "We followed your credit cards, no activity."

"I had a stash of cash," Reeves explained. "I'm an insurance guy. I think about the apocalypse. I'd stockpiled some cash in case we had a big earthquake or something and nobody would be taking plastic."

"And you didn't call the police with your suspicions because…?"

"I own the firm. I bought it, lock, stock and licenses," Reeves answered. "So now I own any violations. I mean…never in a million years would I have thought he'd be killing people. I was beginning to suspect some kind of fraud, y'know, financial stuff. But I wanted to get the files in order before making any accusations."

Wright pressed home his questions. "So again, who is this Dominic guy?"

"Dominic Romero," Reeves repeated, his sadness turning to anger. "It's looking like he had a bunch of policies on people that nobody else knew about. I assume that's what's going on."

So far, Reeves' answers were making total sense. Wright hadn't completely eliminated him as either mastermind or accomplice, but was getting close.

"That's what we think, too," Wright decided to confide. "The insurance company sold policies small enough that claims didn't get reported to the big database. In the company's words their policies were 'under the radar.' We thought it was you who was insuring people and killing them."

"I just bought the place," Reeves exclaimed. "The records are so bad I couldn't have figured out who to kill if I'd tried." He was thinking out loud. "Wait a minute! I just realized…I haven't even owned the place long enough for new policies to take effect. You gotta believe me. I inherited this mess."

Wright was beginning to believe exactly that when his phone rang. It was the sergeant in charge of hitting Reeves' office with a search warrant.

Wright answered the phone without even saying hello. "Please tell me your place hasn't blown up."

"It has and it hasn't," the sergeant said. "No physical explosions, but we've got a dead gal here. Looks like an employee. We're still waiting for the coroner, but we got ID out of a purse on the desk. Driver's license picture makes us pretty sure she was one Melissa Fisher."

Wright turned from the phone. "Hey, Mr. Reeves, do you know a Melissa Fisher?"

"Yeah, she works…for me…" The realization started to dawn on Reeves. "Is she…"

"Stand by," Wright said and went back to the phone, whispering this time. "She works there. What's it look like?"

"First blush you'd think suicide," was the response. "Gun's still in her hand, in her lap. Top of her head's on the wall."

"Any note?" Wright asked. "A confession would be nice."

"There's a sympathy card on the desk. It's addressed 'To the family of Bonnie Shelton.'"

"Okay, well, work the scene and let me know what you find," Wright said. "We're getting surprises here too, you've probably heard."

"Sounds like Reeves is dead, and booby trapped his place," the sergeant said.

Wright corrected him. "The place blew up alright, but Alan Reeves is standing here talking to me. He has some idea of who the dead guy is, and we're listening. Um, look, if our guy— whoever it is—was good enough to make a buncha murders look accidental, then he's good enough to stage a suicide."

"That's what I meant by 'first blush,'" was the reply. "This looks almost too perfect, though I don't want to overthink it. We'll get the crime scene folks out here and work it like a murder, not a suicide."

"Good." Wright ended the conversation and turned back to Reeves.

"I'm really sorry to have to tell you this, but it appears Ms. Fisher is deceased also." Wright didn't say any more than that.

Detectives like to watch the reaction when someone is told of a death.

Reeves bent over, grabbed his stomach, and promptly threw up. "My God, everybody's dead but me," he managed between retches. "Why did he have to kill her? She was just a girl who worked in the office."

Wright had seen a lot of murderers fake grief, but not one had ever been able to fake barfing. Unless the man were to subsequently put his foot in his mouth, Wright was chalking him up as a witness, maybe even a victim.

"Why do you think he killed her?" Wright probed.

"He probably thought she knew too much," Reeves managed to reply. "I actually kept her out of everything. She didn't know crap, in fact she was mad about it."

"What do you mean?" Wright asked.

"She wanted to help sort things out. She kept insisting she could, but I didn't think she was ready. That's why I brought Bonnie back in. She knew the system and had worked on the files."

Wright's next question had to be a little less gentle. "Any chance Ms. Fisher was trying to tinker with the files, or keep you from seeing something?

"What, like she was in on it?" Reeves stood up straight now, his outrage overriding his stomach cramps. "No WAY. She was a sweet girl. She might have had a slightly inflated picture of herself and her abilities, but she was just a girl and she definitely wasn't in on a bunch of murders."

"Mr. Reeves, there are indications that Melissa committed suicide," Wright said. "You know her, we don't. Do you think that's possible?"

Reeves answer was unequivocal. "No. God no. Murder's all it can be. The Melissa I know wouldn't have helped him fake death claims, much less actually kill other people. And she wouldn't have committed suicide."

Lenora Hogan joined the two men just as the conversation was wrapping up.

"Mr. Reeves, we're probably going to have a lot more questions for you in a little while," Wright said. "Why don't you wait in my car for a few minutes? You look like you could stand to sit down."

"Sure," Reeves responded. "But there's no way Melissa was involved in this. I can't believe it."

Hogan offered sympathy. "Sir, this whole thing is unbelievable to all of us. I hope you're right, I really do."

Reeves sat in the passenger seat of Wright's car as the two detectives huddled out of earshot.

"I don't think he's our guy," Wright explained. "First of all, he's alive. I think our real suspect is the dead guy over there."

"Who is he?" Hogan asked.

"Reeves said he's the former owner of his insurance firm," Wright continued. "We'll get the details later, but this is lining up like we thought. The guy ginned up insurance policies and then made the deaths look like accidents. I've got some property crimes guys over at the office who've never worked a murder scene. Can you head over and guide them a bit?"

"Sure…who's dead?" was Hogan's obvious question.

"A girl who worked in the office. Presents as a suicide, but on this case who knows? And get Bryce Finn over there to work it with his dog."

"Why?"

"I don't know why," Wright replied. "But at the very least he's been a good luck charm. He has a habit of finding things we didn't even know we were looking for. I want his eyes, and his dog's nose, on that scene."

"And here?" Hogan pressed.

"Yes, after the rubble cools down. But the dog can't get in here while the rubble is still smoldering, so have him and Sierra work the office first."

"Gotcha," Hogan replied. "I'll call Bryce, and I'll let you know when he's done. If things have cooled down here, he can swing by."

* * *

It didn't take long for Bryce to get to Reeves' office. He was excited about the prospect of being in on the resolution of a case.

"Most of the time we find 'em or don't find 'em, and never know the outcome," he told Hogan. "Thanks for letting me come."

"In the words of Bob Wright, you have a habit of finding things we didn't know we were looking for," Hogan said. "We want you to work this scene to death, pardon the expression. Inside and out. We want to know anything that's here that shouldn't be."

Bryce decided to start outside, along the likely escape route of any possible killer. If Sierra found something discarded, it would weigh against the death being self-inflicted.

Bryce worked Sierra around a dumpster, and along the wall next to the office door. They made a quick lap around the small office building, and on the final side Sierra slowed a bit. She turned and doubled back into the wind—always a good sign—then crossed into some landscaping that served as a border between Reeves' place and the office building next door.

The bushes were very closely planted in that spot, and Bryce couldn't see what Sierra was squeezing into. She pushed through the bushes, stopped, started to sit and got poked in the rear by a thorn. She yelped, jumped ahead and spun around. Bryce hoped over the same bush, and could see Sierra had a swipe of blood across her muzzle. She shook her head, flapped her ears and sat again, staring at the ground.

Right where Sierra was looking, Bryce could see a brown leather jacket. It was dry, shiny and obviously recently-dropped. Across the sleeve was a thick smear of blood, not yet dry. From all appearances it was the same blood now staining Sierra's whiskers.

"I'm really sorry," Bryce blurted to Hogan. "I think she got poked when she was first trying to sit, and jumped. Looks like she smeared some of the evidence on the jacket," Bryce said.

"Not optimal, but no worries," Hogan replied. "If it wasn't for Sierra, we might not have noticed a brown jacket in brown bark dust under brown shrubbery. And it looks like there's still enough of whatever's smeared there to test."

"I'm thinking it's blood," Bryce held out.

"Me too," Hogan said. "But until the lab tells us it's blood it's just evidence. Have you got something to clean Sierra with?"

Bryce carried lots of towels in his rig, and cleaning Sierra up was no problem. But he was confused about why the blood had smeared at all. He was about to bring it up to Hogan when she dialed her phone.

"Bob...it's Lenora. Good call on bringing Bryce out. Sierra found a bloody jacket that almost perfectly matched the landscaping. We'd probably have missed it just looking with our eyes."

"What size?" Wright asked. "Our dead guy here looks like a large."

"Large it is," Hogan responded. "I guess that also means your guy isn't wearing a jacket. You figure he set up Melissa, got some of her blood on him, so he ditched the jacket and headed over to Reeves' home?"

"Well, that's a starting theory anyway," Wright said. "You been inside yet?"

"Headed there now," Hogan said, walking and talking. "We had a little issue with Sierra getting her nose on the jacket, but there's still enough blood to test. It'll probably be the victim's anyway but...does your dead guy have any injuries other than gunshots?"

"Nope," Wright said. "One in the chest and one in the face. Classic SWAT double-tap."

"Okay," Hogan replied. "Then this is probably her blood, not his. It's a crapload on the left sleeve."

"As if the person wearing it had been standing next to someone, forcing a gun into their mouth suicide-style?" Wright asked.

"Pretty much what I'm thinking," Hogan replied. "The cerebral artery gives a couple of final big spurts and the sleeve gets covered. We'll have Bryce look around inside but I think the office is better suited for the CSI types than the dog."

Wright agreed and the two hung up. Walking over to his car, he opened the door and knelt down. "Mr. Reeves, does your friend Dominic own a brown leather jacket?"

"Not that I've ever seen, but we weren't what you'd call friends," Reeves answered.

* * *

The rubble was still smoking when Bryce and Sierra arrived at what used to be Reeves' house. Wright walked up to Bryce's rig before he could even shut off the engine.

"Thanks for coming. The fire laddies say this'll be hot until tomorrow. No way can you get in there now."

"No worries," Bryce said. "The place really is blown to smithereens. We'll come back tomorrow to check it out, but can we talk about something else?"

"I told you if you had ideas, I wanted to hear them," Wright responded. "Whatcha thinkin'?"

"When was the shootout and explosion?" was Bryce's question.

"About two hours ago by now," Reeves guessed. "We can get it pinned down off the radio logs. Why?"

"What time did your team get to Reeves' office in relation to the time of the explosion?" Bryce pressed.

"It was a simultaneous deal, we had planned to sync the raids until the shooting started," Wright answered. "But you're killing me here. What are you thinking?"

"The blood was still wet...on the jacket," Bryce said. "I've been to a lot of scenes, and never soon enough that blood would smear."

"Oh, Lenora told me," Wright said. "You get Sierra cleaned up okay?"

"Yeah, not an issue," Bryce mused. "It's like the opposite of that deal with the cane. We were there soon enough that the blood hadn't dried. Yeah, it was a thick glob, almost like pudding. But it wasn't dry. Lemme ask this: Are you thinking that your dead guy here went to the office first and killed that woman...made it look like a suicide...and then came here to murder Reeves and blew up the house?"

"Well until just this moment, yeah," Wright said. "The timeline...?"

"Seems pretty tight. Stage the suicide at the office, ditch the jacket and boogie over here. Then he had to rig the stove...I assume it was the stove...to blow up and then get in a shootout with SWAT. All quickly enough that when we got to the other scene, the blood on the jacket hadn't coagulated."

"Hogan said it was a crapload of blood," Wright responded, playing devil's advocate.

"It was," Bryce said. He didn't normally discuss the gore he encountered out of respect for the dead and their families. "Imagine a bottle of ketchup poured on your sleeve. There was a hint of a crust where the surface had dried, but underneath was still wet enough for Sierra to smear."

"So you're thinking two people?" Wright cut to the chase.

"It just seems to have all happened too quickly," Bryce explained. "Could one person have been at both scenes so close in time? And he...or they...whoever...must have known you were coming...?"

"What?" Wright was somewhere between shocked and offended.

"Well, he or they decided to eliminate two witnesses and potential evidence literally minutes before you hit the buildings." Bryce said. "That's gotta be one heck of a coincidence...unless they knew the game was up."

"Jesus," Wright exhaled. "We kept a super tight lid on this. Did you tell anybody about our last meeting?"

"Not even Katie."

Chapter Twenty
By a Neck

This would hopefully be the last of them. With Romero dead and Alan Reeves out of hiding, Bob Wright had been able to go through the list of death claims. This body, recently discovered, would hopefully mean case closed on the county's worst-ever serial killings. He looked up to see an unexpected face exiting the coroner's van.

"Hey, what brings you out here, Dr. Jamieson?" Wright asked.

It was indeed unusual for one of the county's on-call forensic pathologists to visit a death scene. Pathologists generally limit their work to the coroner's "operatory," that very sterile place where the dead are examined for clues to their deaths.

"Call me Pete, and it's good to get out of the office once in a while," the tall, gray-haired man responded. "Dex was short of deputy coroners, so I took the oath and occasionally come in to help out. I'm called a 'reserve coroner,' sorta like being a volunteer firefighter."

"Didn't know there was such a program...annnd I won't be signing up," Wright joked in return. "The only thing that helps me tolerate seeing dead bodies is knowing *you're* the one who has to touch them."

"I'll give ya that," Jamieson allowed. "Some days the gloves just don't seem thick enough. Well, with the pleasantries out of the way let's talk about the *un*pleasantries. Whatcha got?"

"Looks like a pretty routine suicide," Wright said. "Gun in the mouth and the entire brain about 10 feet away."

A little known fact about suicides is that when a large caliber handgun is placed in the mouth, the brain doesn't just disintegrate. The bullet itself passes cleanly through soft matter and shatters the top of the skull. Expanding gases from the gun's discharge follow the bullet, picking up the brain and frequently ejecting it as a single unit.

"Ten feet would move him into first place for the year," Jamieson said. "I think the furthest we've charted is eight feet eight inches."

"I don't want to know," Wright said. He'd heard rumors of the "Great Kitsap County Brain Slide Contest" in the coroner's office, and wanted no part of it.

"I do have a favor to ask, though," he continued. "We have a newer dog handler from Search and Rescue stopping by. Name's Katie, and her dog has never been up on a badly decomposed body. This seems like a routine suicide so we'd like to give her the opportunity."

"I dunno," Jamieson said. "After all we go through to protect death scenes, this seems kind of unusual."

"It's not unusual at all, we just don't talk about it much," Wright explained.

Jamieson was not moved. "I just can't see a family being happy that their loved one was used as a training aid for a dog."

"And I can't imagine them being happy their loved one was a contestant in a brain slide contest," Wright pushed back.

"Alright, I gotcha. But the dog doesn't touch the body."

"Totally agree," Wright said, immediately becoming conciliatory. "Katie will walk her dog up, on-leash, and just let it sniff the immediate area. A few inches is the closest its nose will get, and maybe not even that if the dog does a proper alert right away."

"That'll work, I guess," Jamieson said. "I've gotta admit I've always wanted to see one of these cadaver dogs in action. Can I watch?"

"Of course," Wright said. "She should be here in a few minutes and Bryce will supervise. Speaking of Bryce, he's already out checking the scene and it looks like he found something. If you'll excuse me…"

Jamieson went back to the van, appearing outwardly to put on his Tyvek suit and grab a body bag. But he watched Wright make his way over to Bryce and continued watching as the two of them began talking.

* * *

"Find something?" Wright asked, noting that Bryce and Sierra hadn't moved from a particular area for about five minutes.

"Yeah. But why is Jacobsen here?" Bryce asked.

"Jamieson," Wright replied. "He's just helping out. Why do you ask?"

Bryce sighed heavily. "I know what you told me about speaking up, and I probably should have, but I just wasn't sure. Jamieson knew something..." and before Bryce could continue, the conversation was interrupted by a series of tones from Wright's two-way radio. They both leaned in to listen, and heard a sense of urgency in the dispatcher's voice.

"Code Zero. All units, help the officer...officer down. Shots fired at the gas station, Highway 305 at the Port Gamble cutoff."

Wright immediately turned and headed back to his Crown Vic. Over his shoulder he gave instructions to Bryce. "Whatever it is, collect it in a bag and when you're done take it to the Sheriff's Office. Don't let it out of your sight until you hand it to a commissioned sheriff's deputy and don't tell anybody what you found."

Bryce yelled an acknowledgement and started for his own vehicle. He kept a supply of plastic bags there, and would glove up to collect what looked like a note—perhaps a suicide note. He knew he was being trusted with evidence, and didn't want to become the weak link for some attorney to exploit.

"Gotta go!" Wright yelled to Jamieson when he got back to their parking spot. "Shooting just south of Kingston...officer down. I'm hoping we don't need you there. Bryce and Katie can help you bag the body." As he peeled out, his tires left a cloud of dust on the remote logging road where they'd all parked.

* * *

Bryce had returned to his vehicle, put Sierra in her kennel, and was grabbing gloves and bags when someone walked up behind him.

"Hi, Bryce. Good to see you again. Dunno if Bob told you but I'm out here today as a deputy coroner. I guess it's just the two of us."

"Good to see you again, sir," Bryce replied. "Detective Wright asked me to collect some evidence the dog found."

"If it's a death scene it belongs to the coroner's office," Jamieson said. "You really shouldn't be doing that."

"Sorry, sir. I heard the earlier conversation you and Bob had, and I know his position." Bryce said. He'd been told "no" too many times by Hicks, and wasn't going to take it from a stranger. "It's not human remains, and it's not on the body, so it's not yours. I'm going to collect it and take it to the Sheriff's office so they can log it in as evidence."

"You're not to touch that suicide note," Jamieson said, following Bryce back to where the note had ended up. "I'll collect it and we'll take it to the coroner's office as part of the death investigation."

"How did you know it was a suicide note?" Bryce asked. "You just got here."

"Wright told me," was Jamieson's first try. Even Barney Fife could have ferreted out that lie.

"Wright didn't know," was Bryce's response, staring Jamieson directly in the eyes. "He blew out of here before I had a chance to show him."

"I just assumed…"

Bryce pressed. "For that matter, how did you know the gloves Sierra found were in the parking lot at that homeless camp? Nobody mentioned it in the meeting. Now you know it's a suicide note before you've seen it."

"It doesn't matter, or at least it won't matter to you in a few minutes," Jamieson said. He put his hand in his pocket and it came out holding a small semi-automatic pistol. In that split second the entire case came into focus.

"Oh God, it IS you," Bryce said. "I wondered how you knew the gloves were in the parking lot. But why did the other guy...Dominic...need you?"

"I was his backup. I made sure the autopsy findings were what they needed to be. It was close on aorta-man. If Hicks had come in the operatory and looked, he'd have seen there was no flap. And he'd likely have smelled the almonds. The guy reeked."

"Almonds," Bryce mused. "The telltale odor of cyanide. It wasn't a heart attack. You poisoned him."

"Romero did, and apparently used way too much," Jamieson said. "It was a good thing I was around to handle the autopsy. You know, if you all had just left well enough alone, you wouldn't be standing here now with a gun pointed at you. The only thing we did was cheat an insurance company."

"You killed people!" was Bryce's stunned response.

"Everybody dies sooner or later!" Jamieson shouted. Then he lowered his voice to almost a whisper and stepped toward Bryce. "Okay, we made a few people die sooner, but everybody dies anyway. We just tweaked the timing to our benefit."

Bryce worked to make eye contact with his captor, trying to make a human connection. But his eyes kept drifting back to the gun.

"Think this through, sir," Bryce tried saying. "If you kill me they'll know it was you. If you don't kill me, I'll tell them it was you. There's no scenario by which your plan succeeds. You need to start..."

"Cape Verde is how this plan succeeds," Jamieson interrupted. "A stable democracy, great climate, and no extradition treaty with the US."

Bryce had initially wanted to keep Jamieson talking. But things had changed. Katie was on the way, and he wanted the situation over before she arrived. If that meant he was dead and Jamieson had fled, at least she wouldn't be sucked in.

"You know they only catch the dumb criminals, right?" Jamieson rambled. "I'll be off on a plane with a very good-looking ID and passport before anybody even finds your body. They'll eventually figure out who and even where, but they won't be able to do a damned thing about it."

As the killer's words trailed off, Bryce's worst fear came true. In the distance, he heard a car door slam. Katie would find them in a few moments and if nothing changed, they'd both be dead. But Katie's arrival also created an opportunity. Jamieson heard her, and turned to look. His attention was divided...just enough.

Bryce lunged the four feet he needed to close the distance between himself and Jamieson. He'd disarmed an old lady once, but this was a full-grown man with a full-grown grip on the gun. At first contact he shoved the gun to one side, then tried to drive the top of his head into Jamieson's chin. He heard teeth clunk, followed by the sound of a shot going off.

Katie heard it too. She'd been standing by the two vehicles, trying to figure out where everybody had gone.

Bryce had a tough decision to make. He was physically maxed out from wrestling for the gun. He had enough strength left to keep wrestling, or yell a warning to Katie, but not both. Actually, it was an easy call.

"Katie! Run! Get back in your car and leave. He's got a gun." The exertion allowed Jamieson to swing the gun's barrel back toward Bryce. Bryce was pulling on the older man's wrist, and pushing on the barrel, trying to spin the weapon out of his grip. But Jamieson also had two hands, and Bryce's every action was met with a reaction.

"Where are you?" Katie cried back. "Who's shooting?"

"Run, I said!" Bryce yelled, the desperation clear in his voice. "I can hold him off, but you gotta go."

Katie wasn't sure what was wrong, but knew something was. She also knew Bryce hadn't abandoned her when she was facing death. She started moving toward the sound of the struggle, forgetting that she'd already let Magnum out of the car.

Magnum heard the grunts and the groans and somehow his little doggie brain knew a fight was under way, just as his big sister Sierra had once known. The dog beat Katie to the scene and leapt onto Jamieson in what hockey players would call a body-check. As he did, a second shot was fired and Magnum gave off a loud yelp. He stepped back a bit, and then re-engaged full-force, his teeth in Jamieson's side.

A trained dog would have gone for the arm, but Magnum was injured and amped up. When dogs get into fight mode they bite anything nearby, even their owner. Under the circumstances, it was more than adequate for Magnum to have at least sunk his teeth into the right person.

Jamieson continued pulling the trigger, and cussed when the gun wouldn't fire a second time. Bryce could feel what had happened. His grip on the gun had prevented the semi-auto from completely ejecting the spent casing. It was jammed in the ejection port.

With the gun inoperative, the need to take it from Jamieson diminished...slightly. Bryce figured Jamieson would need about five hands to fend off Magnum, clear the jam *and* continue fighting. He decided to switch from defense to offense, taking one hand off the gun and using it to punch Jamieson repeatedly in the face. In the frenzy he heard a loud thunk and his adversary immediately went limp. He looked up to see Katie holding her two-way radio like a tomahawk, blood dripping from one corner.

"I used to gripe that these things were so heavy," Katie said, before launching into an adrenaline-fueled ramble. "I guess I'm glad but what the hell is going on why did this guy try to shoot you and where are the cops aren't the cops supposed to handle stuff like this are you hit?"

"Katie, slow down. I'm okay. Take a breath. This guy is some kind of doctor but he's been in on the killings. We gotta secure him before he wakes up."

"If he even twitches I'll hit him again," Katie said, her adrenaline triggering another run-on sentence. "What is the deal why are you having to catch another killer why aren't the cops doing this?"

Bryce knew if Jamieson moved Katie would indeed smack him again. Maybe several times. He tried again to calm her down. "Honey, we're fine now. Bob Wright had to leave because a cop's been shot up by Port Gamble. Nobody would have guessed that somebody from the coroner's office would be in on the case. Let's get his arms secured before he wakes up. Have you got Magnum's leash?"

Katie's breathing slowed and she fumbled a bit, almost frisking herself and eventually reaching into a cargo pocket. "Here you go…wait a minute, where's Magnum?"

The two looked around briefly and noticed Magnum on his side behind a bush, with a bullet wound on his chest. Katie got to him first. "Oh my God, Magnum…baby…" Magnum just lay still, panting gently. Visibly in shock, he stared at Katie with eyes that in one look conveyed love, confusion and pain.

"Direct pressure," Bryce said, dropping the leash and moving to Katie's side. "I've got some clotting gauze in the truck. You hold pressure and I'll get it."

"TAKE THE GUN," Katie yelled, beginning to lose her composure. "Lock it in the car so he can't get to it.'"

Even though Jamieson was still out cold, the gun was what would kill them all. Grabbing the gun was faster than tying up Jamieson. Bryce made it to his truck in record time and quickly returned with the gauze.

"Okay, this comes in narrow strips and has clotting powder inside. We pack it as far down into the wound as we can get. The goal is to stop internal bleeding. It's not much, but it's all we can do here. You gotta get him to the vet."

Katie gently lifted the dog while Bryce held pressure on the newly applied gauze. As they began moving back toward Katie's car, they heard a rustle. Jamieson was awake and in a flash had Magnum's forgotten leash wrapped around Bryce's neck. Bryce was forced to release the pressure on Magnum's wound to get at the improvised garrote. Jamieson had the leash wound so tightly that Katie could see Bryce's eyelids start to droop. She was stunned when Bryce stopped grasping at the garrote and instead unzipped his coat.

Katie could see the gun tucked in Bryce's waistband. In any other circumstance she'd be angry he was packing, but she knew immediately that hanging on to Jamieson's gun had been a good decision. Forced to set Magnum down, Katie closed the distance quickly and pulled the gun from Bryce's beltline. Killing someone was a big decision, but Bryce's eyes were now completely closed and he was starting to slump. She didn't hesitate to bring the gun up and shoot Jamieson squarely in the face.

The man immediately became dead weight, but the leash was wrapped so tightly around his hands that even in death, his grip didn't release. As he fell backwards, Bryce landed on top, face up, eyes closed.

Katie set the gun aside and began working to free her unconscious boyfriend. She eventually managed to create a small gap on one side of Bryce's neck, and was relieved to see some color return to that side of his face. That gave her time to unwind the leash from one of Jamieson's dead hands and fully release Bryce from his leashly bondage.

But Bryce didn't wake up. Struggling to remain calm, Katie gave him a couple of rescue breaths and slapped his face. Finally, he began coming around.

"Where am I?" Bryce asked, instinctively rubbing his neck. "What happened?"

"Whoever this man is, he tried to kill you," Katie explained. "He's dead now. I shot him."

"Where did you get a gun?" was Bryce's next question, though his memory was slowly returning. "Oh God, Katie, I'm so sorry. I didn't mean for you to have to do that. Where's Magnum?"

"He's over here, but I think we're going to lose him," Katie said in a voice that reflected calm acceptance. She'd saved one love, but was now prepared to lose another.

"No...you gotta get him to the vet. Now!" Bryce said.

"I just shot somebody. I can't go running off. I'm a murder suspect." Bryce recognized the guilt. No matter how much one's head knows a shooting was justified, the heart takes a different path.

"Katie, think," Bryce exclaimed. "You're not a murder suspect. You saved my life. Now you gotta save Magnum's. Remember, he got into the fight and distracted this guy just enough to keep us both from being shot. We owe him."

Katie thought for a second and came to agree. She picked up Magnum, who was still breathing, and started for the car. "You alright?" she asked Bryce.

"I'm fine. There's no cell service here but I'll get on the radio. You get Magnum to the clinic...the one on Silverdale Way. The vet there did time in the Army. He'll be familiar with gunshot wounds. I love you."

"I love you too," Katie managed to eke out. The cloud of dust she raised was even bigger than Wright's.

* * *

"SAR 44, WestCom," Bryce radioed.

"SAR 44, you're on channel one. We're in the middle of a shooting," the dispatcher scolded. SAR members always used tactical channels, and were never heard on actual dispatch frequencies.

"SAR 44 I've been in a shooting too. The doctor is dead. We're on the Green Mountain side of Minard Road, just inside the gate. County 128 was here and knows where we are. I need help."

Wright heard the traffic and interrupted dispatch. *"Radio, start medical for that location...break...44 from 128 where's the shooter?"*

"44...Katie shot him. He pulled a gun and shot Magnum, and was going to shoot us. Katie's getting Magnum to the vet."

Though accurate in every way, the information was confusing to both Wright and the dispatcher. Neither said anything for a moment.

"128 from Car 1." It was Sheriff Patterson, already at the gas station making sure his deputies were properly cared for.

"128, go."

"Car 1, things are good here in Port Gamble. One deputy shot and it's not life-threatening. We're going to hand the investigation over to Bremerton PD so you won't be needed. Let's have you head back to 44's location and get that sorted out."

"128 en route. Radio, did you copy to start aid to that location? It's inside the gate, and right on the boundary of the watershed."

"Radio copies...break...44 age and condition of the patient?"

"44...I don't know his age. He has a gunshot wound to the head. Probably not survivable."

Chapter Twenty-One

In a Cloud of Dust

Katie had never driven like that in her life. She left Bryce in a cloud of dust, and was now pulling onto the hard-surfaced road, still trailing a cloud.

"Ohh, God…I almost hit that guy," she thought. She'd looked left before she skidded off the gravel road and onto the paved street. But her momentum took her over the centerline and almost into a head-on with a car coming from her right.

The driver of the vehicle she'd almost hit turned out to be someone she knew well. Not someone she liked, but someone she knew. The driver made an immediate u-turn, and accelerated. He quickly caught up with Katie, and the blue lights came on.

"Nooo," Katie screamed out loud, "I can't get stopped now!" But then, she kicked herself mentally. If her yelling upset Magnum, his heart would beat faster and he'd bleed out. She had to keep her frustrations in check. Soft voice time. "It's okay, little buddy, we're going to get you to the vet and get you all fixed up."

The blue lights were now as big as airplanes in her rear view. She knew better than to run, no matter how good the cause. Stopping was the only way. But in her excitement, she hit the brakes a bit too hard. She managed to keep Magnum from sliding off the front seat, but couldn't prevent what came from behind.

BANG! was the sound of Hicks' patrol car hitting Katie's rig. It sounded worse than it was, but when Katie looked in her mirror she recognized Hicks, though she'd never seen him in uniform, nor with the anguished look of an at-fault driver on his face. Once both cars were off the road, she flew from the driver's seat.

"My dog's dying up here and you can't even pull us over without completely screwing things up," she screamed. "You should be at the shooting, not running into me. Or up on Menard, helping Bryce."

"Calm down, little girl," was Hicks' response. "What shooting, and what's with Bryce? I've been driving around for three hours, and the radio's as quiet as I've ever heard it."

"TherewasanofficershootingandBrycewasalonewithabodyandtheguytriedtokillhimandIshothim," was all Katie could blurt out.

"WHAT DO YOU MEAN YOU SHOT SOMEBODY?" Hicks hollered, putting his hand on his gun. The look on his face told Katie he thought she was crazy, and maybe crazy enough to kill him.

"That guy from the coroner…James…Jamieson…whatever his name was," Katie managed to sputter. "He was in on the killings and Bryce figured it out. But he shot Magnum and tried to kill Bryce so I got his gun and shot him."

Hicks removed his hand from his gun. "This still isn't making sense. You're going 100 miles an hour down the road after apparently shooting somebody. You trying to escape or something?"

"No, like I said, he shot Magnum. I need to get him to a vet. Here, come look." Katie ran to the passenger side of her car and opened the door. Magnum was still alive, but his mouth was agape and his tongue hanging onto the car seat. He was clearly a very sick dog.

Later, Katie would describe Hicks' reaction as being like "flipping a switch."

"Here, let's get him in my rig," Hicks said. "I can go faster than you."

"Wait, what?" Katie asked. "We're putting him in your...."

"Stop foolin' around and get him the hell in my rig," Hicks barked. "Both of you, in the back seat—here, let me grab his back end."

Katie and Hicks gently loaded Magnum onto the hard back seat of the patrol car, where prisoners normally rode. There was a seat belt, but Katie had no time. She turned to put pressure on Magnum's wound and was slammed into the back of the seat as Hicks peeled out. She was surprised to hear the vehicle's siren come on, and they started passing other cars at breakneck speed.

"Do you even know where we're going?" Katie hollered through the plexiglass partition.

"I assume the e-vet in Silverdale, unless you had something else in mind," Hicks yelled back.

"That's the one," Katie replied. "Magnum seems to be stabilizing a bit. His breathing is more normal."

"You just keep pressure on the wound and we'll get him there," Hicks said. He was still yelling to be heard through the partition, but Katie'd also not heard that particular tone of voice before. Somehow, it calmed her.

The two careened into the vet's parking lot and Hicks pulled the car directly up to the entrance door. Katie's door, intended to contain prisoners, wouldn't open from inside. Hicks popped the handle from the outside, but didn't wait for Katie to get out. He bolted through the front door of the clinic. When he returned, a staff member was with him carrying what looked like a dog-sized stretcher.

"Here dear, let's slip him onto this," the woman said quietly. "It'll support him better. How about you? Are you okay?"

"I'm fine," Katie snapped back. "It's Magnum we've got to focus on."

"I know," she said. "But I want make sure you weren't shot along with him."

"I said I'm fine," Katie repeated. "I get what you're doing but the only way I won't be okay is if we don't help my dog."

Hicks held the door while Katie and the woman from the clinic carried Magnum inside. They didn't stop at one of the usual exam rooms. Katie found herself being led directly to what looked like a surgical suite.

The veterinarian was already there, and in gown and gloves. Through her mask she said "I'm Dr. West. How long ago was your dog shot, and from what angle?"

"I guess it's been about 20 minutes," Katie stammered. "The angle...I guess from the front....we were all wrestling for the gun...he distracted the guy just enough..." and she began to cry.

"Listen to me," the vet spoke to Katie while while continuing his examination. "Just like human hospitals, we don't lose many if they get to us alive. You've done everything right getting him here, and now we're going to take good care of your dog."

Katie continued to cry as other assistants came into the room and began to work on Magnum. She saw what looked like an oxygen mask, and a big needle. She didn't need to see any more.

"You need to step outside now," the assistant told Katie. "We're going to do everything we can for your little buddy. What's his name?"

"Magnum," Katie managed to sob out. "His name's Magnum and he saved my...our...lives."

The vet looked down at Magnum just as the assistant inserted the needle. "You're going to take a short nap, little friend, and then we're going to fix you up." The last words Katie heard as she was ushered out the door were "You're gonna be just fine."

The assistant who'd helped get Magnum out of the car now led Katie back to the lobby area. Katie was surprised to see Hicks in a chair, his head in his hands, obviously crying. "Thank you," Katie said. "I'm not sure we'd have gotten here in time..."

"We have to save him," Hicks blurted out. "I couldn't save my dog, but we have to save yours."

"What...are...you?" Katie started to ask. "Were you a canine handler?" She'd never heard of Hicks losing a dog in the line of duty.

"Nope...never been a handler," Hicks replied, as softly as Katie had ever heard him speak. "I've never told anybody this When I was ten, I had the coolest dog, but one day when I was gone he chewed our couch. My drunk of a dad slapped me around for it, then took the dog outside and shot him. The little guy died in my arms, looking up at me," Hicks managed to eke out, his voice cracking. "Even if I'd had the money for a vet, there was nobody to take us. I couldn't save my best friend, so we've got to save yours."

Chapter Twenty-Two
Something Borrowed

"Sweetie, what are we going to do with you? This is the third time somebody's tried to kill you." Bryce's mother was in that difficult place—happy her son was alive, angry that he'd been in danger.

Bryce and his parents were in the lobby of the Sheriff's Office. He'd just finished being interviewed by Bob Wright

"I know, Mom, but I'm just doing my job as a handler. It's not like I'm deliberately trying to stop bank robbers or something," Bryce said. "I'm really sorry."

Bryce's Dad was quick to mediate. "Son, YOU have nothing to be sorry for. You've done nothing but try to help people and it's almost like that old saying…'no good deed goes unpunished.' But your Mom's right. We can't have you getting in these situations over and over again."

Bryce's Mom tried grasping at straws. "Maybe you could just look for missing live people? This cadaver work is what always seems to go so badly."

"Well, remember the nutty woman who pulled the gun on us last year?" Bryce replied. "They told us she'd be harmless. You just never know how these are going to work out."

"Honestly son, if you were younger, we'd pull you out of SAR," Bryce's Dad said. "But you're old enough to make that decision for yourself. We just hope you'll start being more careful about which searches you go on."

"And I have some questions for that deputy who left you alone," Bryce's mother added.

Bryce could accept being chewed out for what he did, but got heated at criticism of his hero. "How could Bob have known a doctor who works for the coroner would be an accomplice? He had an officer being shot at. There was no reason for him to think anything like this could happen."

"Bryce, relax, your Mom's just upset and I am too," his Father said, resuming his role of mediator. "It's because we love you, and we're very proud of what you do for this community. We just want you alive to keep doing it for a long time."

"Well, that much we agree on," Bryce said. "Can we not talk about this now? I'm still kind of wound up from everything, and maybe this isn't the right time for a discussion..."

"Best idea I've heard all day," his father said. "Let's just put this on hold until we're all over being surprised and scared and upset."

"Good," Bryce said. "But I do have a favor to ask."

"Yesss?" his father replied, eyebrows raised.

"Before Grandma died she told me she gave you something to hold for me. I think I'd like to get it from you."

* * *

As Bryce and family were outside in the lobby, Katie was in a dimly lit room drinking a soda and waiting for Bob Wright to come in. The incident continued churning in her mind, and she couldn't help seeing Jamieson's head jerk back, and the splatter of blood from the other side. She knew she'd be seeing that image for many nights to come.

Wright had put her in what police call a "soft interview room." This was not the typical barren interview room with only a table, hardback chairs, a light and a video camera. The chairs were comfortable, the table round and there were soothing pictures on the wall. There was a knock and the door opened. It wasn't Wright.

"I'm Tony Rojas," the man said. "I'm the attorney for the deputies' union."

Katie was already rattled by the day's events. This introduction confused her even more. "I'm not a deputy, and I'm not in the union."

"Today you might as well be. You know Jason Link, right? Well he's the deputies' union president, and he talked with his board. They agreed, unanimously I might add, that I'll be representing you just as if you were a deputy. No cost…I'm on retainer for the union and this is part of my gig."

"Do I *need* an attorney?" Katie was moving from being confused to being scared.

"Any time you shoot somebody, no matter how justified, you need an attorney. It would be a shame for you to say the wrong thing in an interview and have something blow back on you."

"Okay. Well, what happens now?" Katie acquiesced. Rojas took a seat at the table next to her.

"You tell me everything that happened and everything that was in your mind. It's all attorney-client privileged, which means I can't ever tell anyone what you told me."

"I didn't say 'stop.'" Katie said, jumping ahead in her story.

Now it was Rojas' who was confused. "I'm sorry?"

"I didn't say stop or freeze or drop the leash," Katie blurted out. "I just shot him. Aren't you supposed to warn somebody you're about to shoot them? Bryce's eyes were bugging out and his face was blue and he was passing out. He managed to open his coat and show me the gun just in time."

"The law is reasonable," Rojas said, in as soothing a voice as he could muster. "You said Bryce was passing out?"

"Yes!" Katie answered. "His face was changing color and just as I grabbed the gun I could see him go limp. I was sure he was already dead."

"Then you're fine," Rojas reassured Katie. "a reasonable person would likely agree there wasn't time."

"Likely?" Katie asked, slowly.

"Nothing's ever a hundred percent, but I've been through a lot of police shootings," Rojas said. "We have to look at the scene as you saw it, with only the knowledge you had at the time."

There was another knock at the door, and Wright opened it. "You guys ready? If you need a few minutes I can come back."

Rojas pushed back. "Umm, we might need a little more time."

"I just want this over with," Katie said. She liked Bob Wright but didn't like the situation. "Let's get started. I'll answer your questions."

Rojas reluctantly agreed with his client, and Wright joined them in the room.

"Alright, Katie," Wright said. "There are some formalities we need to get out of the way. I need to read you a statement before we begin.

"Sure," she said.

"As a member of Kitsap County Search and Rescue you were working as an agent of the Sheriff's Office, and we're going to conduct this interview just as we would if you were a deputy," Wright said, looking at Rojas.

"Katie, by order of the Sheriff you are directed, under penalty of insubordination and termination, to answer all questions honestly and completely," Wright began, and softened his tone. "Failure to do so may result in your being kicked out of the county's SAR program."

In law enforcement, there are two kinds of warnings. Best known is Miranda, beginning with "you have the right to remain silent."

Lesser known is the Garrity warning, normally reserved for policy violations and not criminal acts. Garrity is the mirror image of Miranda, and compels answers lest the employee be fired for insubordination.

"Are you su…" Rojas started to ask, and stopped mid-word.

Katie was confused by the exchange, but repeated what she'd said earlier. "I'm happy to answer your questions."

"I know, Katie," Wright said. "But when somebody working on behalf of a government agency takes a life, we try to get everything nailed down as tightly as possible. I might be asking you some hard questions but I'll repeat what I said: you're compelled to answer honestly and completely"

There was now no doubt what Wright was doing. Rojas spoke softly to his client. "Katie, tell him everything, including the part you just told me."

Katie walked Wright through hearing the shot, seeing the fight, and Magnum being shot. She got to the part where Bryce unzipped his coat and she could see the gun.

"I just took it, pointed it at his face and fired," she said. "I didn't give him a chance to drop the leash or anything. I just shot him in the face without a word."

"It sounds like that bothers you," Wright said. "What was going through your mind at the time?"

"That there *wasn't time*," Katie replied. "If I'd taken time to talk him into unwinding the leash we might still have lost Bryce, or had him turned into a vegetable."

"Then that's what I'll tell the Sheriff," Wright said. "I hope your attorney told you there's no requirement to warn. In fact, our deputies are expressly prohibited from firing warning shots. If someone is actually being harmed, you're justified in shooting immediately. That's all there is."

Both Wright and Rojas could see Katie's angst over the lack of warning wasn't a legal concern, and wasn't even logical. She was wrestling with the guilt of having killed another human being.

"It's okay, Katie. It's normal to be upset. We'd be worried if this *didn't* bother you," Wright said. "The Sheriff wanted me to tell you that there's help available, like a counselor or chaplain, at department expense.

But Katie's mind was on to other things. She'd heard the word "justified," and that was all she needed for now. "If we're done, I'd like to get back to the vet and see Magnum."

"How's he doing?" Wright asked, grateful for an opportunity to change the subject.

"Thanks to Waylon Hicks, it looks like he'll make it," Katie said. "You heard he got us to the vet, right?"

"Yeah. Pretty ironic. You two hadn't exactly been on each other's Christmas card lists and he ends up saving your dog," Wright mused.

"He cried," Katie said, looking at the floor. "He was in worse shape than I was."

"Wow, I've been through some pretty awful stuff with him and never saw a lick of emotion," Wright said.

"I probably shouldn't share this, but apparently he had an abusive dad who shot his dog." Katie explained. "He was a kid when it happened but I guess it all came flooding back when he saw Magnum in my car."

"Well, whatever. It worked out," Wright said. "Maybe having a jerk of a dad explains why he's such an ass. But I wonder why he wasn't in Port Gamble at the code zero?"

"He said something about the radio being quiet," Katie said.

"Oh. My. God," Wright exclaimed. "The dip-wad must have had his radio turned down or on the wrong channel. He never heard that a deputy had been shot, but that's the only reason he was in the right place to help you."

"The vet said five more minutes getting there, and we'd have lost Magnum. I don't think we'd have made it without Hicks' lights and siren. I hope that leaving the scene didn't make me seem guilty."

"Will you stop looking for reasons to think you screwed up?" Wright admonished Katie, though with a smile on his face. "Young lady, you took an absolutely crappy, no-win situation, and you won. The right guy is dead, and both your boyfriend and your dog are alive. It doesn't get any better than this. Now go. Go."

* * *

With Katie gone, Rojas and Wright were alone in the room.

"And just what in God's name was that?" Rojas asked.

"Whatever do you mean, counselor?" Wright answered, unable to conceal his smile.

"I almost objected, until I caught myself," Rojas said. "You gave her a Garrity warning instead of Miranda."

"Oh gee, I guess you're right," Wright deflected, still smiling. "I just brought the wrong form in the room and used what was in front of me."

"Bull," Rojas answered back.

Wright continued playing dumb. "I guess it's a good thing Katie didn't say anything incriminating. Nothing I got out of her could have been used against her in court. Any criminal charges would have imploded."

"You risked your career for that girl," Rojas said. "The Sheriff would have had your butt if that had gone bad."

"Counselor," Wright replied, lowering his head and looking Rojas directly in the eyes. "Who do you think handed me the form?"

Chapter Twenty-Three
Article Search

"This is an easy way to get both of you back to searching," Bryce lied. "You've both been to hell and back in the woods and regardless, Magnum needs to learn how to search for articles."

The two were in the woods behind Bryce's house, the place where their love of both dogs and each other had first been cemented.

"Magnum's already pretty good at finding stuff," Katie replied. "He's let me know about backpacks and gloves that our subjects have dropped."

"That's when he's after a live subject, and maybe already in their scent pool," Bryce continued. "But we also get searches to just go find stuff that suspects have thrown. Maybe as they were running, maybe from a car. There's no blood on them, so a cadaver dog won't help. A dog trained to find live people also needs to find inanimate objects that have human scent on them."

Katie was more than ready to get back to searching. She'd been cleared in the shooting. Not only had the prosecutor ruled it justified, the Sheriff gave her a handshake and a coin. Now it was past time to get back on the horse. Her main concern was whether Magnum might start showing aggression toward humans. Sierra had been through a similar event, and had come out fine, but the issue was still in the back of Katie's mind.

A secondary worry was Magnum's health. He'd spent a few weeks recovering from his gunshot wound, and seemed none the worse. He was out of condition, though, just like an athlete who gets sidelined with an injury. Katie would have to start taking him for hikes.

Bryce brought her back to the present. "I've hidden something out there, and it's got my scent all over it," he said. "Get Magnum started and let's see how he reacts to it."

"What command do I give?" was Katie's question.

"Your live find command," Bryce said. "Don't confuse him by making this about cadaver work."

"Alright, Magnum, let's 'go find.'" Katie said, and Magnum never missed a beat. If he was traumatized because something bad had happened in the woods, he wasn't showing it. The two of them gridded the one-acre patch of woods, and eventually Magnum slowed and started to move in one direction. His tail was up, his nose was down, and Katie could hear him snort to clear his sinuses.

Eventually Magnum made his way to a spot that had meaning for Bryce and Katie. It was where she'd fallen the first time she'd done runaways for Sierra. Bryce had helped her up, and it was the spot where their bodies first touched. It was where she'd first kissed the geeky fellow student who all the other girls had called "the dog guy."

"Cue him to sit," Bryce whispered.

"Magnum, sit" Katie responded. Magnum did as told, next to a small box.

"Perrrfect," Bryce said. "Little brother has the knack. Pay your dog."

Katie tossed Magnum his ball, and knelt to begin the play-reward ritual. "Ahh, youse a good boy...youdabestyoudabest." Bryce dropped down so he could join in with belly rubs and butt scratches, and Magnum responded by rolling over on his back, so the belly rubs could happen in earnest. The two leaned over him, using all four hands to make it a party for the dog.

"Looks like he's ready to search again," Bryce said. "He didn't seem tentative at all going through the brush."

"I just want to make sure he's okay finding humans," Katie answered. "And if I have to make a cadaver dog out of him and NOT find live humans, that's okay. I just don't want anybody getting bit."

Bryce was quick to reassure Katie that one instance of aggression towards a human—especially a human who was trying to kill them—was not going to ruin Magnum as a search dog. "Sierra got through it just fine. Both of these dogs are smart enough to know when it's okay to bite and when it's not. Honestly, I'm happy to know he'll protect you if I'm not around."

"Well, I always want you around," Katie said, continuing to pet Magnum but moving her body against Bryce's.

Bryce put his arm around Katie, but his words were anything but romantic. "Are you going to check out the article your dog found?"

"There you go again," Katie said. "I'm being romantic and you're ever the dog geek."

"Check it," Bryce said dryly.

Katie reached over and picked up the box, which, she discovered, had a bow on the outside. She raised an eyebrow at Bryce. "Can I open it?" she asked.

"I hope you will," Bryce responded.

Katie pulled off the bow, and flipped open the top.

"Oh my God!! Is this what I think it is? Where did you get the money…?" She looked up to see Bryce had gone from being on both knees, to one knee.

"It was my grandmother's," Bryce explained. "Before she died, she said she was willing it to me. Her exact words were 'when you're trying to start a life with that special someone, you'll have better things to do with your money than buy silly rings.'"

"Well, now I see where you get your practical side," Katie responded. "Are you going to ask me?"

"Do you like it? We could probably trade it in for something more modern if you…" Bryce prattled.

"I love it. It's beautiful but hellooo…*are you going to ask me?*" Katie feigned exasperation, knowing exactly what was coming.

"Oh, right, I guess I just assumed." Bryce straightened himself on his knee and faced Katie. "Look, we've talked around this since that time you were in the hospital. We're not even out of school, but it's safe to say we're not like the other kids. What we've got is no flash in the pan."

"Mm-hmm," Katie said, a raised eyebrow imploring Bryce to get to the point.

"It's pretty clear we're destined to be together, even if the timing is bad…"

Now Katie raised both eyebrows. "Will you stop putting asterisks and qualifiers on my proposal? This is a girl's big moment, so get to it, buster."

"Right…right. okay." Bryce took a deep breath and started to slip the ring on her finger. "I want to life my spend with you, and I'd be handed if you'd give me your honor in marriage."

"What!?" Katie exclaimed. Simultaneously Bryce spoke up. "I'm not sure that came out right. You know what I mean, right?"

"Say it," Katie said. "You gotta say it as you slip the ring on my finger. Take two…*action!*"

"I'd be honored if you'd give me your hand in marriage," Bryce managed to get out. "Will you?"

"Of course, you big silly," Katie responded. "I decided that a long time ago. But every girl needs to hear the words." She reached out and pulled Bryce to her, letting herself fall backwards on the ground. She kissed him much more deeply than the first little peck she'd given him there. Then, slowly she moved her lips across his cheek to his ear.

In the softest, most romantic voice she could muster, Katie whispered "if that stupid phone of yours rings with a search right now, I'm throwing it in the pond."

Bryce moved his own lips to Katie's ear. She could feel his hot breath on her neck. "I left it in the house. No interruptions."

Katie couldn't help laughing. "Aren't we a pair?" she said. "We should be smooching like crazy and not worrying about a phone. But I guess that means we're on the same mmmmmm."

Bryce had moved his lips back to hers, and silenced her with another deep kiss. The only thing missing was romantic music. Instead of violins, they kissed as passionately as any lovers ever had…to the gentle squeak squeak squeak of Magnum chewing his toy.

Neither of them would have had it any other way.

About the Author:

Robert D. "Bob" Calkins has been a search and rescue dog handler in western Washington for more than 15 years. He currently searches with K9 Ruger, a four-year old Golden Retriever who is Bob's third SAR dog. He and his dogs have responded to everything from routine missing person cases, to homicides, to the horrific landslide that in 2014 swept over homes in the tiny community of Oso, Washington.

He is the author of the Sierra the Search Dog series of books for children and adults.

About the Real Sierra

Sierra was Bob's first search dog, a Golden Retriever with the well-known "Golden smile" and a natural ability to find people who'd gotten lost. She liked nothing better than running through the woods hoping to pick up the scent of a missing person. Her paycheck was a simple tennis ball, and a scratch on the head. She worked with Bob for five years, responding to many missing person searches in and around western Washington.

Other books in the Sierra the Search Dog Series

For Teens and Adults:

Digger – Sierra and the Case of the Chimera Killer

For Middle-Grade Elementary Readers:

Bryce Bumps His Head

For Pre-Schoolers

Sierra Becomes a Search Dog

Sierra the Search Dog Finds Fred

Sierra the Search Dog Saves Sally